MR. DECEMBER

CALENDAR BOYS SERIES

NICOLE S. GOODIN

Mr. December
Published by Nicole S. Goodin
ISBN: 978-0-9951276-7-8

Copyright 2019 by Nicole S. Goodin
All rights reserved. ©
First published December 2019

Cover design by Nicole Goodin
Images purchased from Depositphotos
Editing by Spell Bound

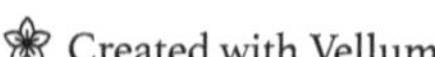 Created with Vellum

For all the babes born in December

1

Lukah

I POUND my fist against the solid door repeatedly. "Let me in, asshole, I know you still live here."

My dad is such a fucking piece of shit.

I amble backwards, unsteady, as I look around for a security camera to flip off.

He's a piece of shit with a nice place at least. There's two cameras pointed in my direction, protecting his fancy-ass pad. I give them both the middle finger, just for good measure.

He's probably in there banging his new wife over the kitchen table or some shit, too busy to come to the door and let his own son in.

Nothing new there. Wife number three doesn't know what the hell she got herself into when she married my douche bag dad.

I smack the door again. Maybe I need a new tactic. He

might not let me in, but *she* might. "Be a good little wife and let me the fuck in!"

I wonder how old this one is. The last one was closer to my age than his. It was actually pretty gross. Absolute fuckin' laugh when she tried insisting I call her mum.

Disgusting old man probably went even younger this time.

"Just a minute!" a female voice answers, and I smirk lazily to myself.

Winner, winner.

Guess I'm going to meet the new Mrs. Andrews in the flesh. What a treat that's bound to be.

The door opens a crack and a set of dark eyes stare at me through the gap, frowning. "Who are *you*?"

I sway from side to side before stumbling forwards into the door.

Maybe Griff was right... that last shot at the club *was* one too many after all.

"I'm not calling you 'Mum'," I say as I push the door, and the chick gasps, scrambling out of the way.

The door swings back and I step forward, colliding with her.

"Oh my god, where are your clothes?" she shrieks.

"What's the matter, sweetheart, the old man upstairs not have a set of abs?" I grab her hand and rub it against my stomach.

She shoves me away, and I stumble into the wall, chuckling as I drop my bag to the ground.

"Get out or I'm calling the police."

I really look at her for the first time. Warm brown skin, dark curly hair and a toned, tight body.

"*Jesus*," I mutter to myself as my eyes rake over her

exposed flesh in those tiny shorts and tank. My dad has even younger taste than I do.

This one doesn't look much older than a teenager, hot as fuck, but young. Way too damn young.

Sick, geriatric bastard.

She tugs her robe closed and glares at me. "Get. Out."

"C'mon, jailbait, is that any way to talk to your new kid?"

She scowls at me, her hands on her hips and her eyes on my chest. "What the hell are you talking about?"

"Dear old dad didn't tell you about his favourite son?" I smirk.

Dad clearly went for looks over brains with this one.

Her eyes widen and her mouth drops open. "Wait, *you're* Lukah?"

"Congratulations. *Ten points* to the new girl," I drawl as I push off the wall, stumble yet again, then clumsily make my way down the hallway to where the old man used to keep a couch.

I'm tired as shit; I don't remember it being such a long walk from the club to this overpriced penthouse. I doubt I'd make it upstairs to a real bed if my life depended on it.

I hear her shut the door and then the padding of her feet on the wooden floor behind me.

"No one told me you were coming."

"Well *surprise*." I throw my arms in the air. "Because here I am."

I drop onto the couch, my Santa hat falling off my head and into my lap.

"Where are your clothes? And what's with the hat?"

I chuckle as I look up slowly at her. She's real fuckin' hot, this one. The thought of my dad taking her to bed makes me want to hurl. I don't know how he gets these women in the first place, let alone gets them to stick around long enough to marry.

"Well?" she demands.

"Well, jailbait, usually when you *strip*, you take clothes *off*."

"You're a *stripper*?" Her voice rises an octave.

"Only on Fridays." I chuckle, my eyes closing of their own accord.

"And the Santa hat?"

"Ho, fucking, ho." I yawn. "It's Christmas, what the hell do you think?"

"Your dad isn't here, you know?"

"Don't. Give. A. Fuck."

In fact, it suits me better if I don't have to listen to him and his bullshit lectures.

"He and my mum won't be back until the morning."

I blink drowsily at her; her robe has slipped open again, showing a slither of skin between her tank and shorts. *Jesus.*

"Are you even old enough to get married?"

"Did you hit your head on the way over here or something? You're making *no* sense."

"I'll tell you what makes *no* sense," I say as I kick off my shoes, "someone as sexy as you, marrying a prick like my dad."

She laughs, a disbelieving laugh. "*Ew.* You think *I* married your dad? No offence, but that's *disgusting*. He's like sixty. How much have you had to drink?"

"Sixty-five," I inform her, ignoring her question, because who keeps track of drinks when they're free? Not me, that's for *damn* sure.

"Whatever. I didn't marry anyone. My *mum* did."

Her mum... my dad... then that means...

"I'm your new stepsister," she confirms, looking all hot and pissed off.

I chuckle groggily.

Stepsister. Yeah right.

I really am wasted.

My brain drifts, sleep taking me. I don't know what the hell was in those shots, but this dream is a new one, that's for damn sure.

2

———

Margot

"I'ᴛ's ɴᴏᴛ ꜰᴜɴɴʏ, B, he's just lying there, snoring!"

My friend Beth laughs down the line as I peer at the stranger sleeping on the couch for the five hundredth time.

"Pics or it didn't happen."

"*Seriously*?"

"You know the rules."

"Urgh, hang on." I groan.

I snap a photo and send it to her before putting my phone back up to my ear. "Incoming."

"Oh. My. God. How bangin' is he!"

"A ridiculous amount." I groan again, my eyes still on the half-naked Santa in front of me. "He said he was a stripper."

"Oh, *girl*, if I had a body like that, I'd be a stripper too."

"You're really not helping, B."

"What do you want me to do? The guy is a crazy kind of hot, I don't know what the problem is."

"The *problem* is that he's turned up here, drunk as hell, and Mum and Rick aren't home. I don't know if I should have even let him inside."

"He's Rick's son, right? Why *wouldn't* you let him in?"

I chew on my fingernail. "I don't think they get along. He wasn't at the wedding, and I overhead Rick telling my mum that Lukah was 'an entitled little asshole with a bad attitude'."

"He forgot to mention the insane set of abs."

I roll my eyes. I *never* should have sent her that photo.

"Beth! Focus."

"Sorry. But could you just touch him real quick? See if they're as firm as they look?"

"I am *not* touching him."

"The old Margot would have," she grumbles. I can practically see her pout from here.

"That's a lie and you know it."

She giggles. "Urgh, fine, no touching, *whatever*. I dunno what to tell you. Can't you just leave him there and go to bed?"

"What if he's not really Lukah? I've never seen a picture, what if it's all some elaborate scheme to rob us? Or what if he's a murderer, and I just let him in?"

"You've been watching too many of those cop shows again."

She's not wrong. I was in the middle of one when Mr. Hello Sunshine here started threatening to break the front door down.

"Whatever, not the point. I can't just leave him here."

"Doesn't Slick Rick have a butler or something? Ask him."

I've told her one hundred times not to call him that, but as per usual, Beth has the memory of a goldfish. One of these days I'm going to wind up calling him that to his face, and my mum will legit kill me.

"He does *not* have a butler, it's just me and the dirty Santa."

"God, I bet he'd be *so* dirty... a body like that..."

"Beth, *c'mon*! I need your help."

She sighs. "Send a picture to your mum? Surely she knows?"

I mull it over a minute. I don't really want to, but I haven't got a better idea, and if he really is a murderer, he could wake up at any second and chop me into little pieces.

I send the same picture through to my mum and within seconds my phone is buzzing with her reply.

Mum: Rick wants to know what the hell Lukah is doing on his couch and where his clothes went?

Well that answers that.

"It's him," I tell Beth. "Phew."

"Good, now feel him up, take a few more pics for me, and go to bed."

"I've never been gladder for you *not* to be here," I deadpan.

"Oh boo." She pouts. "You never let me have any fun."

"I gotta go, B."

"I bet you do." She giggles. "Don't do anything I wouldn't do."

I roll my eyes before ending the call.

Lukah stirs on the couch, his hand rubbing at his bare torso. I watch, totally in a trance as his long fingers trail over each of the ridges of his six pack and then descend lower into the waistband of his shorts.

I dart out of the room as quick as my legs will take me.

I might be telling Beth no, but the truth is, my fingers are dying to explore all that toned, golden flesh.

I need to get a grip.

He's my stepbrother, for the love of god.

No matter how much of a joke I might think this quickie marriage between our parents is, it doesn't change the fact that I'm practically related to that god-looking man on the couch, and that means he's totally and utterly off limits.

———

I WAKE to the sound of music blasting from downstairs; it's so loud I can feel the bass vibrating through the floor.

I open my eyes and peer at my clock; it's only seven in the morning.

For the love of god. The guy was flat-out wasted last night, I don't know what the hell he's doing up already.

I shrug on my robe, making sure I'm covered this time, and check my reflection in the mirror.

I don't know why I care how I look, but here I am, finger-combing my out-of-control hair into a bun and wiping underneath my eyes for left over mascara before creeping downstairs.

The music is blaring from the sound system in the living room, some song I don't recognise, but that instantly makes you want to shake your ass and twist your hips.

Stripper boy has good taste.

I can smell bacon cooking; he must be in the kitchen.

I sneak through the living room, past the couch that

still has his Santa hat sitting on it, and peek around the corner to try and spot him.

Holy shit.

I swallow deeply, purely so I don't drool.

He's in there alright. Every inch of that fine body, right in front of me as he dances in front of the cook top, his hips thrusting and rotating in the most delicious way.

The bacon smells good, but *that* guy, he looks good enough to eat.

"Sweet baby Jesus," I whisper.

He's wearing nothing but a pair of tight grey boxer briefs, and I can't even deal with how sexy his back is.

He sings along to the lyrics as he cooks.

I duck back behind the wall, leaning against it to catch my breath.

This *isn't* good.

I'm not equipped to deal with a guy that looks like *that* – certainly not one whose dad just married my mum, and *definitely* not this early. I haven't even had my morning coffee.

I need to get a hold of myself.

Sure, he's a good-looking guy – absolutely fucking smokin' hot – but he's just a guy.

I can handle hot. I can be cool.

I give myself the pep talk, take ten deep breaths, and stroll into the kitchen as though I'm not acutely aware of every thrust of my stepbrother's tight ass.

"You're up early," I yell over the music.

He turns, a smirk already on his lips as he appraises me over his broad shoulder.

"Well, well, well, jailbait, I was starting to wonder if I dreamed you up."

I cross the room, being careful to keep my distance, and take up a spot at the breakfast bar.

He grabs the remote, lowers the volume of the music and leans against the bench, eyeing me with an expression that makes me nervous.

He crosses his arms across his chest, and I can't help but track the movement with my eyes all the way down the waistband of his boxers.

I would have thought I'd dreamed up that six pack too, if it weren't for the photo on my phone that I've snuck a peek at, at least half a dozen times since I took it.

"Eyes are up here."

I shoot daggers at him as I meet those intense blue eyes that just top off the perfect package he's offering.

"If you don't want people to look, maybe you should try wearing some clothes every once in a while," I say, hoping that I sound as unaffected as I'd like to be.

He chuckles, his mouth stretching into a wide, easy grin. "I'll let you have the show for free this time. Family discount and all that."

He chuckles at my bewildered expression and turns back to his frying pan. "You eat bacon, jailbait?"

"Why the hell are you calling me that?" I demand.

He glances back at me, quirking an eyebrow. "I think it's pretty self-explanatory, don't you?"

"Yeah, if I was fifteen years old it'd make perfect sense."

"Still makes sense at seventeen, sweetheart."

His patronising tone irks me. I know I look young, so does my mum. She says it's a blessing to look years younger than you are, but when you're *actually* young, it's a damn curse.

"I'm twenty-three, asshole. So cut the kid crap."

"Bullshit you are."

"You want to see my I.D?" I deadpan, growing more and more agitated with this guy by the minute.

When I walked in here, he was red-hot sex on a stick, but now... now he's starting to seem more and more like a thorn in my side.

He takes the pan from the heat and carries it towards me, sitting it down on a board on the bench.

"Twenty-three... *no shit*." He chuckles, entertained.

"You know, you're really fucking rude."

"What I lack in manners, I make up in good looks though, don't I, jailbait?"

He's fucking with me; we both know it. He's trying to goad me, but I'm not just some dumb girl he met in a strip club. If he wants to play games, we'll play.

"Correct. You're hot as hell," I tell him, blasé, not giving him any indication that I've spent the past few hours obsessing over the way he looks.

He's silent – *surprised* – for a few beats before laughing loudly like I just told him the funniest joke he's ever heard.

He's infuriating. I'm barely holding on to the self-control not to stomp my foot and stick out my tongue.

"Where's my dad?" he asks.

"Out."

"With your mum?"

I nod.

"She as sexy as you?" he asks as he snags a piece of bacon from the pan and tosses it into his mouth.

"Don't."

He frowns. "Don't what?"

"Don't call me sexy. You haven't even asked my name

and you're already hitting on me shamelessly? You're all class."

He smirks. "Alright, what's your name?"

I narrow my eyes at him, hating his cocky, arrogant presence, and hating myself for craving more of it all the same.

"Margot."

"Lukah."

"I'm aware."

"Well good for you, I, on the other hand, wasn't informed I was inheriting anything other than mum number three."

"Maybe if you'd come around even once in the past six months, you might have figured it out."

He smirks again, but his eyes are hard. "Pass. That'd involve seeing my dad."

He strolls towards the fridge, and I can't help but watch him as he goes. He's pissing me off, but *man*, he looks good doing it.

"And what's so wrong with that?" I question, curious about his cryptic response.

"My old man is a prick."

I frown at him as he takes the bottle of orange juice from the fridge and drinks straight from the top.

Not only is that disgusting, but he's also wrong about his dad. Yeah, I think he and my mum should have waited longer to get married, but Rick is alright. I like him well enough.

He's good to my mum and he's been nothing but nice to me. Even offering to let me crash here in his ridiculously flash apartment until I can get myself a new place after the holidays. Although I guess it's my mum's place now too – she moved in after they'd only been dating a few weeks.

I want to come straight out and ask him why he and his dad don't get along, but I need to stop engaging in conversation with him, like, five minutes ago.

He holds the juice bottle in my direction, offering it to me, and I shake my head, grimacing. "*Tempting*, but no."

"You know forty-seven percent of people drink out of the bottle when they're alone."

"Thanks for the fun fact, but I'll let you in on a little secret, you're *not* alone."

He winks at me, slides the bottle on the bench and reaches for another rasher of bacon. I don't know how often he eats food full of fat, but the fact that he eats like this at all, while looking like *that,* is so totally unfair.

"Bacon?" he offers.

I want to say no, but it's *bacon*. I'm stubborn, not crazy.

I snag a piece, and he grins, like me eating his bacon pleases him.

And now I've just thought about my mouth and his meat in the same sentence and that can't lead to anything good.

"Margot?" I hear my mum call from the direction of the front door, and I almost sag into the bench in relief.

As much as Lukah seems to be enjoying our little match of to and fro, I need a break. He's not playing fair. He's too fucking attractive for this game.

"In the kitchen!" I yell back.

I can hear Rick and my mum talking, and I don't miss the way that Lukah frowns before quickly replacing the look with a smug smile as re refocuses his attention on me.

"You seem relieved they're here, jailbait, what's the

matter? You don't like being alone with me? Afraid you won't be able to help yourself?"

"I'd rather shit in my hands and clap than get it on with you."

His grin widens. "That was a visual I didn't need."

"You're a real cocky asshole, you know that?"

He chuckles. "Try telling me you don't like it. I'll wait."

He's infuriating. I spin on my stool, giving him my back, but like the bastard I'm learning he is, he doesn't give up that easy.

He's in front of me before I even realise what's going on, his narrow hips sliding between my parted thighs and his toned torso right there in front of me, his hands planted against the bench on either side of my body.

I suck in a breath as the bulge in his underwear presses against my sleep shorts.

He leans in, his lips brushing the lobe of my ear. "Still waiting, jailbait."

The rebuttal is right there on my lips, begging to be set free, but I can't make it happen. I'm completely tongue-tied. Rendered speechless by his bangin' body.

I shouldn't, but all I can think about is touching him, having him touch me.

"What the fuck are you doing?" Rick's booming voice comes from behind Lukah, and just like that, the spell is broken – my brain reboots.

I try to scramble back, shoving him in the chest as I go, but he doesn't budge so much as an inch.

"Oh my goodness." My mother's voice follows as she no doubt stumbles upon the same scene her husband just has.

Lukah just laughs, his warm breath tickling my skin as he pushes off the bench, away from me.

"Long time no see, *Dad*."

Rick's face is less than impressed, and my mum's eyes are nearly falling out of her head as she appraises Lukah from head to toe.

I know, right? I feel like saying, but it really wouldn't help the situation in the least.

Rick is decent looking, for an old dude, but Lukah is just... there aren't words.

"What are you doing here?" Rick demands.

My mum clings onto his arm. "Rick, honey, he's your son, he's always welcome."

Lukah smirks. "Yeah, Dad, what Mum, version three-point-o said."

Someone makes a noise of disbelief. It might have been me.

It's becoming clear that Lukah Andrews has zero fucks to give.

My mum, bless her heart, continues, undeterred, holding out her hand towards Lukah. "It's so good to meet you. I've heard so much about you. I'm Kate."

Lukah raises an eyebrow but takes her hand and shakes it anyway. "If my old man ever spoke to me, I might have heard something about you too."

Rick is still shooting his son a death glare. It's incredibly uncomfortable to watch.

I don't know what the story is between these two, but there doesn't seem to be any love lost between them whatsoever.

"I'll ask again, what are you doing here?" Rick grinds the words out.

Lukah shrugs a shoulder. "I was in town."

Rick strides across the room and flicks on his huge,

fancy coffee machine that I haven't even attempted to use yet.

"When are you leaving?"

"*Rick*." Mum scolds him before turning to Lukah. "Are you staying for the holidays? We'd love it if you would. I'd really like to get to know you."

I breathe in deeply through my nose. The last thing I need is for this guy to be spending any more time here than he already has.

I'm on Rick's side with this one, I need Lukah gone. As soon as possible.

"You know what? I *was* planning to head back on Sunday, but staying for the holidays sounds fun, right, *Margot*?"

He caresses my name with that stupid, sexy voice of his, and I curse the day my mother ever met Rick Andrews.

My stepbrother smirks at me, and I smile sweetly in return. "Can't think of anything better."

3

Lukah

New mum isn't quite as hot as her daughter, but the apple sure didn't fall far from the tree.

I guess it's lucky the eye candy will be worth it, because apparently, I'm sticking around this hell hole a while longer.

It's the absolute last thing I feel like doing, but there's just something about pissing off my dad that I can't walk away from.

"It's settled then," Kate announces gleefully. "You're staying for Christmas."

I don't know what she's so thrilled about. If she'd have come home about five minutes later just now, I bet she would have found me and her little girl in a much more compromising position. Bet she wouldn't have been so happy then, but whatever, I don't give a shit. As long as my dad is pissed, I'm happy.

I grin at Margot and she scowls at me.

That girl wants me like a fat kid wants cake.

Two weeks with her is going to be really god damn interesting, because here we are, one big happy fucking family.

"I'll just make myself at home in my old room."

Dad mutters something under his breath and I chuckle.

I don't even have an old room here. I've crashed in one of the several guest rooms over the years, but the old bastard has never offered me a room to myself. In fact, he's never once even offered to have me stay.

"I'll bring you up some fresh sheets and towels," Kate offers.

I want to rip the piss out of her little hostess act so badly, but it's not her fault she married a wanker. I mean, I guess it kind of is, but she's not the one I've got a problem with. *He* is.

In fact, I could see myself getting very friendly with my new step mum, that would piss Rick off more than my shitty attitude and uninvited presence ever could.

"Pretty *and* kind, you got yourself a good one here, Dad."

"Oh god, *shoot me*," Margot mutters under her breath before sliding her sexy ass off her seat and strutting it out the door.

The curve of her ass in that robe is almost too much for my self-control.

This is going to be one hell of a holiday break.

"She seems sweet," I say, barely restraining my laughter as Margot hears and flips me off as she stomps up the stairs.

"She is, so you stay the hell away from her," Dad snarls, coffee in hand and death glare in his eyes.

"Oh c'mon, old man, you need to learn to share. That's what you always taught me, right? That *I* should share."

His eyes narrow and neither of us says a word.

Kate is the one to break the silence, clapping her hands together once. "Well I'll go and hunt out that linen," she says as she rushes from the room, leaving me and my dad alone.

Prime moment for some quality father son bonding time.

"If you're going to be in this house, you'll play by my fucking rules."

"I'm twenty-six years old, not eighteen, I don't give a shit about your rules."

"You start by wearing a god damn shirt," he carries on, ignoring me. "And if I catch you in your underwear anywhere near that girl again, you'll be out on your ass."

I chuckle humourlessly. "What are you going to do, Dad? Cut me off? You're about six years too late for that threat."

"Just keep your dick in your pants and we won't have a problem."

I laugh, arrogantly. "He's not going to have any fun in there though, is he?"

He sets down his cup and takes a step towards me that is meant to be menacing, but I'm taller than him these days, and I stopped fearing him a long time ago. "Stay away from Margot, *and* from Kate."

"What's the matter, old man? Worried your woman might prefer a younger model?"

I've got absolutely zero fucking interest in banging his

wife; his stepdaughter, however, is an entirely different story, but he doesn't need to know that.

"You fuck this up for me, and so help me god–"

I chuckle, cutting off his rant, and walk away, leaving the last of my fucks back there with him.

I don't need to mess this up for him – he'll take care of that on his own. Always does. Doesn't mean I can't have some fun while I sit back and watch the show though, and Margot, she's got fun stamped across her forehead.

I snag my costume off the floor of the living room, my bag from the doorway and head up the stairs.

I find Kate in the biggest of the spare rooms, fluffing around, doing mum shit.

I drop my stuff onto the bed, and she turns to face me.

She's clearly uncomfortable with my half-dressed state, but to her credit, she doesn't say a word about it.

She's clearly got more self-control than my dickhead dad.

"So, fresh sheets are on the bed. Towels are here. I'm sure you know where the bathroom is."

"Kate," I say, refraining from telling her to chill the fuck out, "I'm good. You don't need to make a big deal out of doing shit for me, I can take care of myself."

"You're right. Sorry. I guess... I just thought... I mean, we haven't met before and I wanted to make a good impression."

I give her a smile. Poor woman looks like she's about to shit bricks. "You've made a good impression, much better than the one I'm sure I've made on you, but I'll tell you what, let's just pretend this morning never happened and start over."

"That sounds great, your father is just tired, we were out late and–"

"You don't want to start doing that, trust me, Kate," I say grimly as I turn my back on her and grab a towel from the neatly stacked pile.

"Doing what?"

I glance at her over my shoulder. "Making excuses for the way Rick is with me, not unless you're in the market for a full-time job."

She frowns at me, not understanding, but she just needs to give it some time, she'll understand soon enough.

If Dad hasn't shown his true colours around her yet, he must be about due.

I drop my boxers to the ground, and leisurely wrap the towel around my waist. She rushes from the room, calling back, "We'll chat more later."

I chuckle. Anyone would think she hadn't seen an ass before.

————

"Yo, LA!" Griffin yells across the club to me over the pulsating beat.

Don't know who he thinks he's yo-ing, trying to sound all street gangster... the dude is a white boy from a rich home. The only street he's familiar with is Sesame Street.

I tip my chin at him and cross the empty club to see what the boys are up to.

This is where I was performing last night. I haven't danced on this stage in months, but as long as I keep my rig in good shape, Griff is good with me dropping in for one-off arrangements.

I'd say it was a surprise having my best mate wind up owning a strip club, but all you'd have to do is check our high school year book, or watch the end-of-year video of him taking his uniform off in front of hundreds of screaming students, and you'd know it was destined to happen.

Helix and Conrad slap my palm as I stroll past them – they're both prepping their routines for tonight's show. Fridays are huge, but Saturdays are insane.

That's when the freaks come out, the bachelorette parties, the twenty-first birthdays... if you want to make some serious cash, you do it on a Saturday.

"Come back for round two, LA?" Conrad asks as Griff kills the music.

"If this clown will let me." I tip my head in the direction of the boss man.

My home crew of boys have called me 'LA' since we were twelve. It's nothing more than my initials, but guys are pretty unoriginal around here, and all these boys have picked it up like a bad habit.

"You keen for another spin, pretty boy?" Griff asks, his excitement catching.

"Might even be around for the next couple of weeks if you've got a spot for me?" I grin.

When I started this, it was nothing more than a way to pay my way through law school without having to rely on my dad and his money.

It only took one time up on this stage and I was hooked.

Everyone thinks this gig is about the girls, the booze, hell even the drugs if you want them, and that plays its part – I'm not going to lie about the amount of times this job has got me laid, but there's a bigger high than any of that when you're up there, and nothing else in my life comes close.

"No shit?" he asks, practically bouncing with energy.

"No fucking shit, man, I got roped into spending the holidays with Dad and his latest broad."

"Old man Andrews strikes again." Griff chuckles. "That dude can't keep it in his pants any more than I can."

"At least you're smart enough not to put a ring on any chick that gets your dick wet."

The guys all laugh.

Griff throws his arm around my shoulders and leads me away from the group. "If you're serious, I could really use you the next couple of weeks; Christmas is always fucking crazy and Kev had to go home to spend time with his grandad or some crap, so I'm a man down."

"Consider yourself back up to full numbers. I haven't got shit to do around here. May as well make some money."

He squeezes my shoulder and bounds off, full of fucking vigour, as always. Even hungover as hell, that guy is always pumped. We always said he had ADD or something.

"Oh... that chick from last night left her number for you after you bailed," he calls from across the room, and I follow after him, intrigued.

"Which chick?" I ask when I find him out back, surrounded by raunchy costumes and ridiculous props.

"You're cocky, bro, I like it." He chuckles. "The *chick*, the one with the birthday party, blonde, huge rack..."

"Oh, Jesus. That's a no from me," I reply as I help him lift a box to the other side of the room.

"Dude, she was hot."

"They're all hot, but that one had crazy eyes."

He chuckles. "What kinda eyes are they?"

"The kind that say 'I want to get married and have your mini stripper babies', *that* kind of crazy."

He howls with laughter. "She was barking up the wrong tree with you then."

That she fucking was.

"So when do you want me back?"

"Shit, man, if you're ready to take your gear off, I'll have you back up there tonight."

I smirk. He should know by now that I'm always ready to take my gear off. "I'm in."

"Fair warning though, tonight is going to be crazy, Deb double booked us with bachelorette parties, and I said yes to a Christmas party about a hundred years ago and never wrote it in the book, so it's going to be crazy packed."

That's classic Griff right there. It's a wonder he manages to keep this place operating.

"The more the merrier."

4

———

Margot

I THINK one of my ear drums just burst.

A whole bunch of my mum's oldest friends turned up about an hour ago, every one of them wearing ridiculous pink feather boas, penis straws on cords around their necks and a variety of other sashes and badges.

They look like the bachelorette section at the discount store threw up on them. *Violently.*

"This is so hilarious." Beth giggles as she snaps yet another picture of my mum being dressed up with a veil, garter and every type of penis merchandise ever made.

I think these women woke up and thought they were twenty years old again this morning.

I think they've also overlooked the fact that mum is married already, and that they should have had this hot mess of a party *before* she tied the knot, but there's no convincing them. This thing is happening regardless of how much I complain, and so far, that's a fair damn bit.

"This is *something* alright." I wince as one of them laughs in this awful, high pitch tone that reminds me of an animal squealing.

"Who died and took your soul with them?" She gives me a sassy side eye. "You have to admit, this is pretty funny. Your mum looks ridiculous."

"Can't argue with that." I giggle, shaking my head as she sips a cocktail from her penis straw and shakes her hips.

"*You* need a cocktail." Beth shoves one into my hands and I take it gratefully. If we're going to do this thing, I'm going to need alcohol. A *lot* of alcohol.

"So... is hotty-mc-hotness around?" Beth asks, making a show of glancing around.

Honestly, I thought that would have been her first question when she walked through the door.

"*Nope.*" I shake my head. "He dropped his pants in front of my mum, got into an argument with his dad and then bailed. Hasn't been back all day."

"Your mum is so lucky." She sighs dreamily. "He's probably out doing sit-ups and pleasuring women. Maybe even at the same time."

I almost spit out the mouthful of my drink. "Oh my god, can you not?"

"You were thinking it."

"I can assure you, I was *not.*"

"Do you have his number? We could totally drunk dial him later."

I don't have his number, and I couldn't be happier about that right now – calling Lukah when I'm under the influence of Miranda's famous cocktails would be the complete opposite of a good idea.

I can barely contain myself around him when I'm sober, no matter how cocky and infuriating he is.

"He's a stripper, B, I wouldn't touch him with a ten-foot pole."

"Well I'd totally be down for a stripper, just saying."

"Yes!" Veronica, one of Mum's friends, yells, overhearing our conversation, "let's go to the strippers!"

Jesus Christ.

"That's not what I said!" I point out, but it's too late. I said the word out loud and now the universe is mocking me.

"Strippers! Strippers! Strippers!" they start chanting.

"Oh, this is *so* good." Beth holds up her phone, videoing them. "I *love* your mum's friends."

"There is no way in hell I'm going to the strippers with my mother."

"You'll do what you're told, party pooper."

"Ladies!" Miranda calls out, trying to be heard over their chanting, "what kind of best friend would I be if I *didn't* book my girl in to see some hot guys shaking their asses… Guess what, bitches? We're going to the strippers!" She does a dance as she makes her announcement, and I can't help but laugh.

"This is literally the best day of my life," Beth says.

"This is literally the worst day of mine. I'm not watching my mother get a lap dance. I *will* hurl."

"I'll watch her." Beth smirks. "Might even get one for myself; if they look anything like your new brother, then I'm *so* in."

God me too, I think, but don't say, because there's wo way I'm admitting that out loud.

If I never think about Lukah Andrews' rock-hard abs again, it'll still be too soon.

I desperately need a distraction.

Maybe this night could be what I need. Maybe I need to go and see some crazy-hot guys who *aren't* my new step-brother and have about fifty more of these cocktails while I'm at it, to take my mind off him.

My mum catches my eye and giggles, her cheeks flushed with excitement. "Come on, go-go, it might be fun..." she calls across the room.

I roll my eyes.

"Fine," I grumble to Beth. "I'll go, but if some dude sticks his junk in my mum's face, I'm out."

WE GET SHOWN to two tables, right at the very front, up close to the stage.

This isn't going to end well; I can feel it. This is going to end sweaty and embarrassed.

The girls insisted we have the taxis stop on the way so they could get cash out. They've been discussing in great depth where the most appropriate place is to tuck the money into and I don't remember laughing this hard, ever.

I hope these dudes are ready for this.

I sit in the seat furthest from the stage. There is no way in hell that I'm going to be one of those chicks that gets dragged up on stage for all to see. Beth can do it; she's *buzzing* about this whole thing.

She grins at me as she sits down, her own fistful of cash clutched in her hand.

I shake my head at her in amusement as I down the drink I was given on my way in.

I can feel the cocktails now, the alcohol is warming me from the inside out, loosening me up.

Another drink appears in front of me, some fancy cocktail with a slice of fruit and an umbrella sticking out the top.

I sip it and moan in appreciation of the sweet, fruity taste. *Pink gin*. This stuff is the devil's juice. You can't even taste the alcohol in these things and then before you know it, you're falling down the stairs.

"Bring out the cock!" Beth yells as the lights start to lower and the room fills with cheers.

Definitely the devil's juice.

"Oh my god." I giggle. "You're going to end up fucking a stripper if you don't calm down."

She winks at me. "You know what, I've just added that tasty idea to my bucket list."

"I'll take you to the doctor when you catch an STD," I promise her.

"Thanks, Mum."

Music starts playing, and as much as I didn't want to come here in the first place, I have to admit, this gets your heart pumping. I'm humming with excitement as the lights go down.

The beat drops and a tall, dark-haired, handsome-as-hell guy slides out from behind the curtain. He's wearing street wear, a hoodie and grey sweats. The whole thing is very *Magic Mike*, and I'm *so* here for it. He's *incredibly* hot.

I never would have thought that getting drunk with my mum and her friends and coming to the strippers would be exactly what I needed.

The girls all start cat calling, along with the rest of the

room as Mr. Abs-to-burn starts stripping off, all the while working it like his life depends on it.

It doesn't take long before he's got the hoodie off, his sweats slung low on his hips and his hat backwards on his head. The smirk on his face assures me that he knows exactly how good he looks doing this.

"Oh, I could totally be persuaded to sit on his face." Beth leans into my ear and shouts over the music.

I erupt into laughter.

"Didn't anyone ever tell you that they save the best for last? Don't peak too early."

The guy leaps off the stage, grinds his crotch against a few screaming women before making his way over to our table.

I cover my eyes as he loses the pants and shakes his ass in Miranda's face.

Miranda looks like she's enjoying this far too much as she stuffs notes into his thong.

"Oh my god!" I squeal through fits of laughter.

I knew sitting in the front like this was going to make us a target. I grab my drink and down the rest of it; something tells me I'm going to need it.

"Best. Night. Ever!" Beth screams as he moves on to her, lifting her clear off her seat and into his arms, her legs draped over his shoulders in a move that gets me far more hot and bothered than I'd like to admit.

Beth winds up on her back on the stage, cheering and laughing as he rolls his big body into hers suggestively.

I cover my mouth, trying to contain the fits of laughter.

This is *too* good. It might be the alcohol talking, but I'm *really* glad we came to the strippers after all.

"I think he just got me pregnant." Beth breathes

heavily as she's deposited back into her seat with a wink from her half-naked friend.

He waves goodbye and struts backstage, a bunch of cash stuffed into his barely-there underwear.

"Oh my god, that was the funniest thing I've ever seen."

She sips her drink and fans her face. "I'm not going to lie to you, I think I enjoyed that a little bit too much."

"I think I enjoyed that just the right amount." Miranda giggles, her cheeks flushed.

I glance at my mum. She's having a great time, drinking and laughing with her friends. As long as one of these guys doesn't get her up on the stage and give her a lap dance, I think we'll be just fine. There are just some things a daughter does *not* need to see her mother doing.

"And now for something... *festive*..." the hot guy with the mic announces.

I turn back to the stage just in time for a remixed version of jingle bells – jingle *balls* – to start playing, and to see a group of five men wearing Santa hats come out onto the stage.

"Oh no, no, no, no, *no*," I whisper.

I already know what I'm going to find as I check their faces, one by one.

The last one to get into position, right there on the end with the hottest body I've ever seen.

My freakin' stepbrother.

5

Lukah

Well this is unexpected.

The last thing I anticipated when I came out from behind that curtain was my brand-new step mum and her mind-blowingly hot daughter, but sometimes life just throws you a bone.

Literally.

I should care about the half boner that I'm rocking from just seeing her here, but I guess these girls are just going to get a bonus show tonight. Even mummy dearest – because that's not the most god damn awkward thought I've ever had cross my mind, but fuck it, it is what it is. She is here, after all – in a strip club.

I smirk.

Margot, sweet, *sweet,* Margot is staring at me like she's just seen a ghost.

I wink at her as I dry-hump the air, imagining that it's

her the whole time. Then I drop to the floor with the other lads and do the same thing, never once taking my eyes off her.

I've got to give her credit, I expected her to look away, but she's holding strong, watching my every move with an intensity that makes it really fucking clear she's imagining herself underneath me too.

The chick next to her leans in and whispers something in her ear, Margot nods, and I very clearly see her mouth the words 'well fuck'.

I smirk at her, cocky as fuck, as we work our way through the routine, the hordes of woman screaming at us.

I'm down to just my underwear and my god damn Santa hat now – nothing Margot hasn't seen before, but being alone in the kitchen with her doesn't compare to her eyes on me in a crowded room. It's erotic – I can picture all too vividly taking her right there on that table.

Conrad back flips off the stage and heads into the crowd, weaving his way through the screaming women, Helix slides his hat onto the head of some chick that's cheering and having the time of her life.

The other two guys find themselves girls too and then it's just me on the stage, with only one place to go.

Her.

I chuckle, and her eyes widen as the realisation of what's about to happen hits her.

That's right, jailbait, I'm coming for you.

I leap off the stage, prowling towards her in a way that should make her fucking scared.

"No, no, no!" she squeals as I approach.

"Could this night get *any* better!" Her friend cheers as

I grab Margot's chair and tip it backwards, catching it in a well-practised move before her head hits the ground.

Nope, I don't think it could get any better. Stripping is a great time normally, but this is just the icing on the top of the cake.

The chick that's given me a hard-on from the moment I laid eyes on her, has her head between my knees, and I'm not sure I could think of a better place for her right now.

I find Kate and wink at her. She's beyond shocked to see me here; I don't know if that's because the old man was too embarrassed to tell her this is what I do for money, or if it's because I'm about to lift her little girl's face into my crotch.

I do exactly that, lifting her into the air, the chair coming with her as she squeals and clings onto it for dear life.

"Put me down!" she yells as I carry her up onto the stage and sit her back down, right way up.

This isn't part of the routine, the guys normally make the rounds of the room, teasing girls, getting tips and playing up the act before disappearing out back, but this is too good of an opportunity to pass up.

Griff is always up for the guys doing a bit of improvisation, so I'm rolling with it.

Joel is in the DJ booth and he never used to pass up the opportunity to pump out a beat for a spontaneous lap dance either, so hopefully he's still got my back.

Margot stares at me with wide eyes, her hands gripping the chair so tight her knuckles are white.

"Relax, jailbait." I smirk.

She jumps off the chair, trying to make a run for it, but

I'm too fast for her, I press her back into it, laughing as she mutters, "oh, sweet Jesus," under her breath.

I've got her hands trapped in mine, and I grin widely as Joel drops a beat for me.

Just like old times.

I press her palms against my chest, and she squeezes her eyes closed tight.

"You've been imaging this since you found out I was a stripper," I tease, as I lower myself into her lap, "admit it."

"Bite me," she grinds out.

"I charge extra for that." I chuckle.

Her eyes spring open as I shove her hands down to my stomach.

The chair goes flying and she's on her back before she even registers the move.

I grin as I dry-hump her entire body, pressing her into the floor.

"Oh my god," she cries, but this time she can't hide her smile as she tries to cover her eyes with her hands.

She's enjoying this. My little jailbait is a *dirty* girl.

I rear back, and in one move, flip her onto her stomach and pull her ass against my crotch.

I can't last long like that, it's too easy to imagine the real thing.

She shrieks as I put her on her back and continue teasing her the best way I know how.

The crowd is going wild as the song ends and I get to my feet, holding my hand out to help her up.

She takes it, her skin flushed and her breathing laboured. I know how she feels. That was hot, even by my standards.

The boys jump back up onto the stage, high-fiving me as they head out back to get ready for their next act.

I lean into her ear. "Wait for me after."

It's not a question, it's an order.

She nods her head, just one tiny movement, but it's enough for me.

———

"So *that was new*. That what they been teaching you at law school?" Griff chuckles as I reach for a bottle of water.

"Saw an opportunity, couldn't let it pass me by," I reply between swigs.

"Not gonna lie, bro, got me a little hot under the collar," Conrad jokes.

I flip him off, chuckling.

"Who was the chick?" Griff presses. The guy is like a bloodhound. If there's a story to be had, he'll sniff it out.

"That's my brand-new stepsister." I chuckle.

Griff spits out the mouthful of water he just took, showering us all.

"Dude! The water routine isn't until last."

"You're going to fuck your *sister*?" Griff demands.

"She's not my fucking sister, dipshit, it's not incest."

He points a finger at me as the boys laugh. "*Bro*. She's your sister."

"My dad banging her mum doesn't make us related. Chill."

"Sister fucker." He howls with laughter, slapping me on the back. "I thought shit might get loose having you back, but I had *no* idea."

"You saw her, right? Can you blame me?"

"Not even one little bit." He whistles low. "Hell, I'd probably fuck her if she was my sister too."

"Can we stop talking about who's fucking their sister

and get fucking ready for the next number?" Helix throws me a firefighter's helmet, and I catch it with a grin.

Just like the good old days.

I don't push my luck by going near Margot again, but every time I dance on that stage, I can't take my eyes off her.

"Off to bang your sister?" Griff chuckles as I head for the door after my last number.

"If I get lucky."

"At least there's no awkward chat about whose house you'll go back to." He grins.

I flip him the middle finger and push out the door.

The show is still going, but I'm done for the night.

I scan the front row, but the dark eyes I'm searching for aren't there.

I find her at the bar, sipping on a cocktail, her eyes darting around the room every few seconds, hopefully looking for me.

I take in her short skirt and tight-fit top.

She's a walking wet dream; perky ass, lean legs and a rack that makes me get hard on sight.

I skirt around the stage, not missing the way women's eyes linger on me even now that I'm clothed. I might not do this as often as I used to, but I'm accustomed to the seductive looks certain chicks give you after a show. Hell, I spent six months of my life sleeping my way through women like that.

There's nothing wrong with a healthy sexual appetite or a woman who knows what she wants, but banging random chicks doesn't do it for me like it used to.

One of the other boys can take those willing and eager participants for a roll in the hay, I've got other plans.

I stalk towards Margot, watching her and her friend laugh and whisper between themselves.

It looks like it's just the two of them now. Hopefully Kate had the good sense to run before she really saw something she didn't need to see.

It's not every day you can say you stripped for your dad's new wife, on what looked like a belated bachelorette party, but hell, life is wild like that.

The friend sees me coming and whispers to Margot, who searches, finding me and tracking my movements until I'm standing right in front of her, pressing her back into the bar.

"Jailbait," I murmur.

"Trouble," she replies, and I grin.

"Beth," her friend chimes in. "But I'll take a sexy nickname if you or any of your buddies want to throw one my way."

I glance at her out of the corner of my eye.

She grins.

I hold my hand out to her. "I'm Lukah."

"Oh, I know who you are." She smirks as she shakes my hand. "But more importantly, who was your friend from the first dance? He started something I wouldn't mind him finishing."

"Griffin." I chuckle. "He's a buddy of mine, owns this place."

She fans her face. "Rockin' bod *and* a businessman. Is it too early to talk marriage?"

"It's not too early to talk *fucking*," I offer with a shrug.

"Offer me a deal I can't refuse, why don't you?" She smirks.

"Oh *lord*." Margot groans, pulling my attention back to her.

I've got her effectively trapped against the bar, her back pressed against the cool metal and my feet planted on either side of hers.

"Having a good night, jailbait? Where's your mum?"

She clicks her tongue. "I think you scarred her for life. She's never going to be able to look you in the eye again."

"It's just a body, babe. I bet she liked the show."

"*I* sure as hell did," Beth replies, unashamed as she drains the last of her drink.

I glance at Margot's drink, it's empty too.

"Hey, Mickey!" I call over her shoulder to the bartender, "get these two another round, on me, and I'll take a beer."

He nods at me. "You got it, LA."

"Let's do some shots!" Beth suggests, but Margot cuts her off.

"You can't bang a stripper if you can't stand up straight."

"Who needs to stand up?" She grins lazily.

I chuckle. This chick sounds like a handful.

"Where's your friend anyway?" She pouts. "I've been waiting."

I glance around behind me and wave Griff over when I spot him being cornered by some chick that looks old enough to be his mother.

He shoots me a grateful look and heads our way after brushing her off.

"Oh yay!" Beth claps her hands together. "Introduce me? Do you think he'll like me?"

Fuck's sake, I didn't come over here to play cupid, I came here for the woman in front of me. I turn my attention back to her and she gasps as I step closer, our hips pressing together.

Griff claps me on the shoulder, and I grunt out an intro.

"Griff. Beth. Get acquainted."

I watch Margot, watching as Griff leads Beth a few feet away to a seat.

"Jailbait," I growl.

She gasps, her eyes slowly shifting to meet mine.

"You waited."

"You told me to," she breathes.

I smirk. Fuck yeah I did.

I run the back of my fingers from her cheek down her neck, shoulder and arm, all the way to her wrist. "You enjoy the show?"

"Some parts more than others," she replies, her tongue darting out to moisten those full, pink lips of hers.

I press my hips firmer against hers. "I bet I can guess which parts."

Her eyelids flutter closed for a second before slowly opening again. "You're *trouble*."

"You're damn right I am," I growl, my hands landing on her hips and digging into the soft flesh beneath her clothes.

"I steer clear of trouble." She practically pants.

"Good fucking luck with that, jailbait. I'm going to be everywhere you look," I rasp.

I dip my head, running my nose down the length of her neck and nipping at the hollow of her throat.

She sags forward, gripping my shoulders with her hands.

"*Trouble*," she says, her voice a moan.

"Inevitable," I correct her.

6

———

Margot

WALKING into an apartment with my stepbrother's arm around me is probably all kinds of wrong, morally and every other way possible – but the things he's doing to my insides feels so damn right.

I've had too many cocktails to care, and he's downed enough beers that even if he had a problem with this before – though I'm certain he didn't – he wouldn't give a flying fuck now either.

I should feel embarrassed; it's glaringly obvious what we're here for, at Griff's place at one in the morning, but I don't. Truth is, if Lukah didn't get me to a bed soon, I was going to combust with all the sexual tension.

I don't even like the guy. He's cocky and conceited, arrogant and stubborn, but my god he's gorgeous. He's the kind of guy you can't decide if you want to punch or screw... if you want to knee him in the balls or drop to your knees and give him the ride of his life.

I sure as hell know which options I plan on choosing tonight.

Apparently we're not the only ones with sex on the brain. Griffin and Beth have been all over each other for hours. B was giving her own stripper moves a pretty good crack as Lukah led me out of the living room and into a spare bedroom, closing the door behind him.

He leans back against the door, watching me as I back up towards the bed.

"I've been thinking about fucking you *forever*."

I raise a brow at him. "I bet it's been a really long twenty-four hours for you."

He pushes off the wall, taking me roughly in his arms. "Jailbait gives backchat, huh?"

"You bet." I smirk, finding my confidence now that we're alone. This is nothing I haven't done before. He might tease me about looking young, but what I lack in that department, I more than make up for in others.

I know exactly what this is – a one-night stand – one that's going to be pretty fucking awkward come tomorrow, but I don't care.

He's hot, we're drunk, and I want him.

I'll worry about the awkwardness around the Christmas tree later.

"What else do you give?" he taunts me.

"Want me to show you?" I ask, licking my lips.

He drops his head back and groans, "Woman of my fucking dreams."

"Any woman willing, is the one of your dreams."

"Don't act like you know me."

"But I *do* know you. You're cocky, smoking fucking hot. You think with your dick. Anything I've missed?"

He tugs me against him, and what was flying at half-mast in his pants earlier is standing at full attention now.

"*This* dick?" He smirks.

God, I'm probably going to hate myself for this when I wake up in the morning, but not even self-loathing will be enough to stop me from doing it anyway.

I'm dying to know if he's got reason to be this arrogant.

"Where's those fancy moves from earlier?"

"You want me to dance for you, or do you want me to fuck you?"

"Maybe I want both."

He tugs his shirt over his head and my fingers are drawn to the defined ridges like gravity.

"If I give you both, you'll want to marry me next."

I pull my own top over my head. "Not going to happen. *Trust me.*"

"Promise you'll still hate me in the morning?" he growls as he drags his jeans down his legs.

"Like my life depends on it," I agree as I strip off my tiny skirt and drop it to the floor.

"I bet you'll be begging me for more."

"I'll be too busy despising *everything* about you."

He grabs my hand and forces me to feel his rock-hard dick. "Even this?"

"Maybe not *that*," I reply quickly, my pulse skyrocketing at the feel of him in my hand.

Jesus Christ, this is going to be one hell of a night.

He leans forward, his teeth grazing my ear as he unsnaps my bra with all the precision of an experienced playboy.

I hope he learnt some good tricks from all those

women, because I'm going to demand every single one of them.

I'm confident he'll deliver; he's already got me feeling weak in the knees, and he hasn't even kissed me yet.

He lowers his head, turning his attention to my nipples and my head falls back, a moan coming from my lips.

"Bet you'll be asking for more of that too, *jailbait*."

"You sure talk a lot for a dude with such a big dick. You not know how to use it?" I taunt him, desperate for more.

He scoops me up under my ass and throws me onto the bed, his body coming down on mine in the next second in a move so hot it should be illegal.

"Oh, babe." He chuckles arrogantly. "You're about to find out."

———

I WAKE up in the morning with a pounding head, but a satisfied smile.

I have to hand it to the guy; he knows his way around the bedroom.

He also knows his way around the shower, kitchen bench and the floor in the hallway just outside the room, but that's not the point.

Those killer moves from the stage, seductive and sexy, translate *unbelievably* well in bed.

Sleeping with a stripper has never been at the top of my to-do list, but now that I've tested those waters, I might have to make a habit out of it.

Jesus, the man can move.

If Beth had even half the night I just had, she'll be begging me to hit up the strip clubs on the regular.

There was this one move, I don't know what you call it, but it blew my mind. Just thinking about it has me needy.

"Fucking hell," I breathe.

"You got that right," Lukah's husky voice comes from next to me.

His hand snakes out under the sheet and caresses my stomach, and given all the places he's become well acquainted with on my body these past few hours, I shouldn't have a problem with this, but it's morning now, the sun is up and my morals have arrived with it.

I twist away from him and swing my legs over the side of the bed, reaching for the first item of clothing I can get my hands on – his sweatshirt. I shrug it on and tug it down to cover my ass as I stand.

"Don't go getting all shy on me now, wild child." He tosses off the sheet, completely unashamed of his morning wood as he gets up and stretches his hands high above his head, showing off every single muscle in his flawless body.

"Put that thing away."

He smirks. "First complaint about it that I've heard from your mouth."

"Well you better get used to it. We had a deal."

He laughs, but reaches for his boxer briefs, stepping into them, casual as hell.

Jesus Christ, tight grey underwear does absolutely nothing to dull the appeal of that thing.

"That deal was bullshit and you know it."

I exhale heavily. "That deal was *legit*. We had fun, and now I can go back to thinking... no *knowing*, you're a player who takes his clothes off for a living."

"Don't lie to yourself, jailbait, there's no way we're not having a repeat of last night." He talks smooth, *seductive* as he crosses the room, coming closer to me by the second.

I step up to meet him, my finger jabbing him in the chest. "Thanks, but no thanks. I tested the goods and I *don't* want to buy."

"Liar."

"Asshole."

"Princess."

"Prick."

He chuckles, his boyish grin too fucking cute for a mouth so filthy.

I arch a brow. I mean what I'm saying. It doesn't matter how sexy he is. A repeat performance is not on the cards.

He shrugs, backing away from me, every muscle in that perfect body flexing and stretching as he gathers our clothes off the floor and throws them on the bed. "If that's the way you want it."

"That's *exactly* how I want it."

He makes a show of rearranging himself in his boxers, my eyes focusing on his hand without permission.

He shrugs on his t-shirt, his jeans following. "You want to put some clothes on? Or have you changed your mind already?"

I point at the door and he chuckles, strolling towards it like he has all the time in the god damn world.

"Wait... I think I'm forgetting something." He points to my body and my eyes lower to the item of his that I'm still wearing.

"I know where you live, I'll bring it back," I reply.

He crosses his arms across his chest, his head shaking, eyes alight with amusement. "Yeah... I think I'll take it *now*."

Fucking *asshole*.

I shake my head at him. "Dickhead."

"Chicken shit."

Fuck him, he's not winning this game.

I tug the sweatshirt over my head, stroll across the room naked as the day I was born, place it in his waiting hand and turn back around, giving him a full view of *everything*.

"Fuck me," he mutters, his voice gruff.

"Already did," I quip.

I don't turn back around.

I hear him leave the room chuckling. Only then do I let myself smile about the whole encounter.

Lukah Andrews is three things for certain...

Sexy as hell, a god in the bedroom, and absolute, undiluted *trouble*.

7

Lukah

"WHAT UP, SISTER FUCKER?" Griff smirks as he strolls into the kitchen.

"You keep calling me that and I'm going to have to dig up some fifth-grade shit about you kissing your cousin."

He chuckles, his expression looking like he's up to no fucking good.

"You drive a hard bargain, LA, but you got yourself a deal."

"Pleasure doing business with you," I drawl.

"So where is the sexy, *Margot*?" he tries and fails to make her name sound exotic.

"She stormed out after telling me to 'eat dick'." I chuckle.

He frowns at me. "I don't get it, you two playing some kind of love-hate kinky shit?"

I take a bite of my toast, smothered in peanut butter. "We're not playing anything. Chick really doesn't like me."

"Tough break."

I smirk. "She'll be back. She just likes the chase."

"She sure seemed to like you last night... several times, if my ears were hearing right."

I punch him in the arm. "Dude, it's fucking weird when you listen to me having sex."

"Stop having it at my place then." He laughs.

I pull the orange juice out of the fridge and get two glasses down. "Do I need a third?"

He shakes his head. "Nah, that little pocket rocket shot off about an hour ago."

"She get those bucket list items ticked off?" I grin.

Beth was *very* vocal at the club about the items she wanted to get completed.

He grins a sly grin. "She sure did. Even added a few more in the moment."

"You owe me."

"Yeah, *I* owe *you* for all the free drinks in my club *and* the overnight stay in my spare room that I'm going to have to coat in sterilising spray."

I chuckle as I leave the kitchen. "Might not want to eat off that spot right there if that's how you feel," I tell him, pointing to the place where I bent Margot over the bench.

"Dude!" he yells. "Not fucking cool!"

"I can assure you, bro, it was *very* fucking cool," I yell out from down the hallway.

"You're a shitty mate."

"Yeah but I'm a shitty mate who got laid last night."

There's silence for a few beats. "*Yeah* you are. Virtual high-five, buddy."

I just laugh, but I'd bet my education on the fact that he's high-fiving the air right now.

I strip the bed and toss the sheets in the washing machine, but that's as good as it's going to get from me. If Griff wants to get his hazmat suit on and spray the place down, he's on his own.

I yell out a goodbye and head out.

I'm dying to get home and see how Margot is going to play last night off.

The excitement is killing me.

She walked out of here with a sway in her step and a sassy fucking attitude, but I know better. I see the look in her eye. I know the way I affect her physically.

I'm too fucking old for games like cat and mouse, but the fact that she doesn't even know she's playing makes it too damn appealing to walk away from.

I slip into the apartment with the key I raided from the bowl by the door. My dad is too much of a prick to give his own son a key, but fuck him, I'll just take what I want – his stepdaughter included.

I grin to myself as I think about last night.

She blew my mind. She might come across as sweet and innocent, but I know better now – she's anything but.

If I were looking for a girlfriend – which I'm *not* – I'd want one just like her. She's the right amount of sass and sweet, rolled into the sexiest package I've ever stuck my dick into.

The living room is empty, but I find Kate in the kitchen, drinking a cup of coffee. She nearly chokes on a mouthful of it when she sees me standing in the doorway.

"Morning." I smirk.

"Lukah, hi," she says, searching for words.

"Good night?" I ask as I stick my head in the fridge.

She giggles nervously. "It was... um... *eventful*."

I chuckle. "Bet you didn't plan on seeing your stepson up on stage."

"You know what, I absolutely did not."

"Well I won't tell the old man if you don't," I offer as I cross the room.

"You got yourself a deal."

I grin at her. It's a shame my dad is such a dick, Kate seems alright. Spending time around her wouldn't be too much of an effort.

Her daughter on the other hand...

Speak of the devil.

I watch with interest as Margot dances her way into the kitchen, ear buds in her ears and a towel twisted up on her head.

Her freshly showered scent wafts into the room, bringing back memories of the same smell faintly clinging to her skin last night as I drove myself into her, over and over again.

She hasn't seen me yet, and I'm enjoying watching her, because I'm certain when she does see me, the claws are going to come out.

I know she wants me again; she just doesn't like to admit it to herself, but it's fine with me. I'll be here waiting when she figures it out.

"I think it might be time that I ask you why you're looking at my daughter like that?"

I smirk at Kate. "If you haven't had the birds and the bees talk by now, I might actually feel sorry for the old man."

She raises her brows at me. "Annnnd now is the time I tell you that she's off limits."

It's funny, she doesn't feel very off limits from where I'm standing.

"I know how young men like you operate, and I–"

"Men like me?" I question, interrupting her.

"Men like *you*," she continues, undeterred by me calling her out on her assumptions. "You're a stripper, Lukah. I was young once too. I've met plenty of men who behave the way you do. Sex, no strings. But Margot isn't like that."

The old, *I was young once too* speech.

I almost laugh. I don't think she knows her little girl as well as she thinks she does.

I'm just about to fill her in on *exactly* how much Margot likes sex with no strings, when the woman herself spins around, her eyes landing first on her mum and then on me.

She freezes mid-move, her hand rushing to pull out her ear buds. "How long have you been standing there?" she demands of me, totally ignoring her mother.

"Long enough to know you shouldn't sing."

She looks shocked for a second, before realising I'm fucking with her. "I *wasn't* singing."

I wink at her. "Sweet moves though."

"Perve."

"Cock tease."

"Player."

"Ball buster."

"Alright, that's enough of that," Kate cuts in.

I grin and Margot does her best not to join me, but she doesn't fool me – I know she's enjoying this as much as I am.

"Why don't you two just walk in the opposite direction of one another," Kate suggests.

"Will do. I need a shower anyway," I say.

"Yeah, you do." Margot shoots me a sassy look.

I sidle up next to her, speaking low so Kate doesn't hear. "I'd rather stay here and argue, but I've still got your scent all over me, jailbait, among other things."

Her eyes flutter closed before popping back open to taunt me. "Better make sure you brush your teeth too then." She smirks, smug as shit, because she knows *exactly* what my mouth's been up to.

I chuckle, backing away and heading up stairs.

This girl is going to give as good as she gets, and I couldn't be more ready for it.

———

"Still the same old shit with your dad?" Griff asks as he spots me on the bench press.

"Same shit, different day. Actually, different wife too, but nothing new there."

"He still riding you about the stripping?"

I press the heavy weight up, resting it on the holder when I'm done. "He hasn't said a word about it. In fact, he has barely said a word to me about anything."

"Bet he'd have something to say if he knew about you and Margot."

I chuckle. He certainly would.

"He doesn't even know I'm in law school."

He frowns at me as we switch places. "For real? You've been there, what? Three years now?"

"I'd have to have tits and an ass for him to give a shit about what I do."

"How can he *not* know?"

I watch carefully as Griff presses the bar up into the air before lowering it back to his chest.

"He doesn't want to hear it. He's got no idea I only started stripping for cash for school. When I took those couple of years off to save up, he got it in his head that taking my clothes off was the only thing I was ever going to be good for, and he doesn't listen to anything else."

"No offence, dude," he grunts as he manoeuvres the bar back onto the holder, "but your dad is a prick."

"Been saying it for years."

"You should fuck his wife, that'll really screw with him," he suggests as he jumps up.

I chuckle. "Tempting."

"But let me guess... you'd rather keep playing games with the younger model."

"I can tell you about one hundred things I'd rather do than play games."

"I should have brought a paper and pen."

I grab a kettle bell and plant my feet in front of the mirror for squats.

I blow out a breath as the weight strains my muscles and burns my legs.

"I think you like this chick." Griff grunts as he does the same exercise next to me.

"Yeah, I like her. Last night was insane."

"So, it's just about the sex?"

"It's *just* about the sex," I reply. "What the fuck else would it be about?"

"I think it's about *more* than just the sex."

"You should try thinking less, you'll give yourself a headache."

He tries to flip me off and drops his kettle bell in the

process. It only just misses his foot as it sails to the ground.

I squat again, my thighs screaming in protest. *"Careful."* I chuckle.

"Is it time for you to go back to school yet?" he grumbles.

"Afraid not, you're stuck with me until Christmas."

"At least I get to make some money off your ass." He grins.

"You're basically my pimp."

"I *am* your pimp. Better watch your attitude or I'll put you out on the corner."

"Only if you'll buy me fishnet stockings and a fur coat."

Helix chooses that moment to join us at the weights, catching the end of our conversation.

"Do I even want to know what the fuck you two are talking about?"

We both chuckle.

"I'm not dressing up like a chick, dude," he tells Griff, his expression concerned as his eyes bounce between the two of us. "I know my limits, and that's a hard one."

Griff howls with laughter. "Better cancel that order I had for size twelve men's heels then."

Helix can't tell if Griff is fucking with him or not, the poor bastard. The look on his face is priceless.

"Come hold pads for me, I need to sweat out all that alcohol from last night."

Helix nods, eager to get away from Griff before he gets any more fucked-up crossdressing ideas.

"Pretty sure you sweated it out all over my apartment," Griff grumbles as I strap a pair of boxing gloves to my hands.

I jab him in the shoulder and jog off after Helix.

Most of the guys get sick of working out so hard. It's a tough gig keeping your body in this kind of shape, but I love it.

It gives me complete control over something in my life, and between law school, my dad and all the other bullshit going on – sometimes I just need that.

Helix slaps the pads together and holds them up for a combo.

I hit the pads over and over, as hard as I can until I'm gasping for air.

"Nice, bro, take a break before you spew. I'm tired just watching you."

I clap him on the shoulder in thanks, before doubling back over again to try and catch my breath.

"Big plans for your night off?" he asks.

I shake my head. I've got nothing on the agenda. Nothing other than going back to Dad's place and going another few rounds with Margot.

Just the thought makes me grin.

8

———

Margot

THERE'S a knock on the door of the room I've been using, and I turn, expecting to see Lukah.

I'm disappointed when the man in the doorway is the older version, not the one I've been desperately trying to avoid, yet thinking about nonstop.

"Rick, *hey...*"

"Do you mind if I come in?"

I shrug. "It's your house."

He cracks a smile and enters the room, pausing to look at a few of the framed photos I have on my dresser. Most of my stuff is jammed into a storage unit, but I brought these with me for some reason.

Me and my mum, me and Beth, and some from school.

There's even still one of me and my ex.

He picks up that one. "Boyfriend?" he questions.

I sit down on the bed. I don't know what's made him come in here, but he's clearly in no rush to come out with it.

"Ex-boyfriend," I reply.

He nods and puts the frame back in place.

He glances at me, somewhat uncomfortable, and I actually feel sorry for him. Part of me wonders if it's about my mum. They moved things along so fast, it worries me that they don't know each other well enough.

"Is everything alright?"

"I just wanted to have a chat, about you... *and Lukah.*"

I narrow my eyes as he sits down next to me. That's not at all what I was expecting him to say. Rick has barely seen Lukah and I sharing the same oxygen.

"I'm not sure what you mean by 'me and Lukah', I only just met the guy."

And yet, he's seen every part of my entire body... been inside me...

I decide to keep that little piece of information to myself. The last thing Rick needs to hear is all the ways his son pleasured me, and *god,* did he pleasure me.

He clears his throat. "Kate mentioned some... *tension* between the two of you. She thought it might have been flirting."

"It wasn't."

It definitely was.

"Are you sure?"

"One hundred percent."

Not at all.

"I don't even know the guy, and I know he's your son, but he seems kind of full of himself." I shrug a shoulder.

And with good reason.

Lukah Andrews is the kind of guy who makes

promises that border on being threats with no more than a cocky expression, but I know first-hand that he can make good on those promises. Really, *really* good.

"Lukah is…" He pauses, choosing his words. "He's an entitled asshole, if I'm being honest."

"Don't hold back on my account."

"He's got a problem with authority and he expects everything to be handed to him."

I don't know if he expected *me* to be handed to him, but I pretty much served myself up on a shiny silver platter.

For the first time since I woke up this morning, I feel a tiny pang of regret.

"I'm really not sure why you're telling me this… I mean, I can't imagine we're going to be spending a lot of time together. It's clear you two don't get along so I doubt he'll be hanging around."

"I just want you to be careful."

He lays his hand on my knee, and I have to stop myself from shoving it off.

He's my stepfather now. He's trying to play his role, be a 'dad' to me, but honestly, I wish he wouldn't.

It feels kind of creepy.

"I just would hate to see Lukah take advantage of such a sweet young woman like yourself."

It's lucky I'm more than capable of taking care of myself then.

"Thanks, but I'm fine. You've got nothing to worry about."

I slide away and stand, his hand dropping to the mattress.

I don't know why, but suddenly, I just want him out of here. I don't want his hand on my thigh, or his ass sitting on my bed. In fact, I don't want him anywhere near me.

I'm being ridiculous, I know I am. Rick is a decent man, and my mum is right down the hall – but I've never needed a dad, and I'm certainly not looking for one now.

He gets to his feet, a heavy sigh leaving him.

"Just be careful, and if there's anything you need, or want to talk about, you know where to find me."

I nod, one sharp jerky bob, a fake smile plastered on my face.

I'm absolutely one hundred percent confident that I'm *not* going to be taking him up on that offer, but I don't want to rock the boat by telling him that.

Now is not the time to be a bitch.

The last thing I want is to stuff things up for my mum because I'm reading too much into an innocent gesture.

He leaves the room, and I'm left wondering why I feel like I need a shower.

I watch the empty doorway for a few beats before flopping down on my bed, my heart racing.

I'm overthinking. I know I am. I'm tired and hungover. I've never functioned well on less than a solid eight hours.

I close my eyes and let my mind drift to the reason I'm so god damn tired.

Lukah.

Last night was easily the best sex of my life. Hands down, no competition. But that's all it'll ever be, and it can't happen again.

I had my one night, fucked him out of my system, and now I need to get on with ignoring his obnoxious ass.

"Dreaming about me?" a voice says, and for a moment I wonder if I *am* dreaming, because it's *his* voice.

I frown and he chuckles. My eyes fly open as I sit up straight, already glaring at the intruder.

My heart is racing again, only this time it's out of excitement, not disgust.

As much as he shouldn't, this man gets me all tied up in knots.

"Did I look like I was having a nightmare?"

He pushes off the door frame he's leaning lazily against, and strolls into my room as though he doesn't need anyone's permission to enter.

At least his father had the manners to ask.

I narrow my eyes at him as he takes his time, strolling around, yet looking at nothing but me.

I hate the effect he has on me. If he's going to keep looking at me like that, it's going to make it really fucking hard to keep my hands off him. And that's exactly what has to happen. We had our fun and now we need to move on. For our parents' sake, if nothing else.

"Taking your clothes off tonight?" I ask, my tone sassy.

"Is that an invitation?"

I roll my eyes. "What do you think?"

He chuckles. "Well, based on last night, I'd say *hell yes*."

He prowls towards me, and I hold up a hand to stop him, my fingers colliding with his toned stomach.

"It's a no."

"I do private shows, I'll even give you one on the house."

"I bet you say that to all the girls."

"Nope." He shakes his head, his eyes alight with amusement. "I usually just ask for my two hundred bucks."

"*Two hundred* bucks?" I demand. "*That's* what you get paid for a private dance?"

"That would be a bargain, jailbait."

"That would be daylight robbery."

"I bet you wouldn't be saying that if you saw the goods."

"I've seen the goods, thank you very much."

He smirks, a fucking cocky smirk that makes me want to do something to wipe it off his face, but before I get the chance to do anything at all, he turns, leaving me hanging and calls back over his shoulder, "Meet me in the media room in half an hour."

"Like hell." I flip him off, but fuck my life, because I'm already checking the time.

———

I STOP JUST inside the room, my hands on my hips and a wary expression on my face. "What do you want?"

His eyes lift to mine and his mouth curves up into a grin.

"You know, I prefer you stripped bare, but those pyjama shorts are a close fucking second, jailbait."

"If you're just going to hit on me, I'm leaving."

He chuckles. "I'm definitely going to hit on you, but sit your ass down, we're watching a movie."

"Do you think we're friends or something?" I demand.

"We're step siblings who have sex, but sure... *friends* works."

I scowl at him yet find myself crossing the room and sitting down next to him anyway. "*Had* sex."

"Huh?" he asks absently as he messes around with a remote control.

I huff out a breath. "We *had* sex, not we *have* sex."

He smirks, his focus shifting back to me. "Whatever helps you sleep at night."

I can tell you one thing, having him sleeping just down the hall sure as hell isn't going to help me sleep.

"You're infuriating."

"And you're irresistible, jailbait, now shut that pretty mouth and watch the god damn movie."

"Asshole," I mutter.

"Tyrant."

I cross my arms tightly across my chest and turn my attention to the screen.

It's some action movie that I haven't seen and would probably love, but I can't focus. Every time he moves, I twitch, waiting for him to touch me.

"Stop being so jumpy."

"Stop moving around."

He chuckles as he swings his arm across the back of the couch behind me.

"Am I making you nervous?"

"You'd like that, wouldn't you?"

He doesn't answer me, instead leans in close, the shadow of hair across his jaw scraping my skin.

"Do you want me to touch you, Margot? I could take the edge off real good."

My lids flutter closed as his warm breath tickles my neck and his scent envelops me.

It would be so easy to say yes, to let him do wicked things to me... to make me cry out in pleasure again.

Yes. God yes.

"No," I practically pant.

"That no sounded an awful lot like a yes, jailbait."

He reaches for me, his thumb dragging across my bottom lip. I open my mouth, sucking it in.

He groans. "Fuck."

I want him, god I want him. But this is such a horrifically bad idea.

We're not drunk and at a club. This is his father's place. My mother's now too.

If my mum knew I was down here thinking of all the ways I'd like her new stepson to fill me up, she'd disown me.

I release his thumb and turn to him, my hands already clinging to his shirt, and his weaving their way into my hair.

"We can't," I whisper.

"We can."

"We're family now."

"You should have thought about that before."

"I was drunk."

"You weren't *that* drunk. You want me. Admit it."

He drags me closer.

"You're wrong," I breathe.

Lies.

He couldn't be more right.

"I want you so bad, it hurts," he growls.

"That's only because you can't have me," I whisper, but even *I* don't believe what I'm saying. I'm about two seconds away from begging him to take me right here and now.

He slams his mouth to mine, his kiss like torture of the best kind, making tingles race up and down my spine and daring me to take it further.

I'm just about to climb into his lap, when he pulls away abruptly, chuckling.

He kisses the end of my nose. "Make no mistake, jail-bait. I *can* have you. And I will. But I'll do us both a favour and wait for you to beg."

He lets go of me, leans back against the couch and goes back to his movie like he didn't just steal the breath clean out of me.

Smug dickhead.

Just like that, he's back to being a total maddening prick.

I only wish that didn't make me want him more.

I grumble a string of curse words under my breath and consider bolting, but fuck him. I'm not running. I'm going to sit right here, *not* begging him to touch me, and take a small amount of satisfaction from seeing the bulge in his shorts that he's making absolutely no effort to conceal.

I smirk to myself. I certainly didn't win that round, but I'm not prepared to say I lost it either.

9

Lukah

"Wʜᴀᴛ ɪs ᴛʜᴀᴛ ʜᴏʀʀɪғɪᴄ sᴏᴜɴᴅ?" I groan as I push the door open to Margot's room.

I'm all for loud music, but this isn't music, this is torture.

She smirks at me, her long legs teasing me in her cut-off denim shorts.

Sexy fucking bitch.

She mouths the words to the god-awful Christmas carol as I rub my temples.

Last night was a big night. I wasn't even meant to be working, but after the night prior, where I found myself kissing Margot and then promising to wait for her to beg, I decided I needed to get out of the house.

I needed some kind of release to stop myself watching the hours tick by on the clock.

Waiting is the exact opposite of what I want to do.

I want to grab her, strip her bare and fuck her senseless, right here in her room with the door wide open, surrounded by fucking tinsel.

"It looks like the South pole threw up in here."

"*North* pole, moron," she corrects me.

She carries on, totally undeterred as I drop onto her unmade bed and lie down, wearing nothing but a black pair of Calvin Klein's.

She turns around to grab another length of ridiculously shiny shit and falters, her eyes landing on me.

"You better have showered after last night."

"Why?" I smirk.

"Because I don't want to catch an STD from lying in my bed."

I chuckle. "I think if I was going to give you an STD, it would have happened when I stuck my dick in you, but whatever."

She doesn't have an answer for that.

I chuckle as she snaps around, going back to her decorating.

I roll over onto my stomach and breathe in the smell of her, all over her sheets.

She smacks me with a pillow. "Can you not?"

"What?"

She swirls her finger at me. "Be in here, looking like *that*."

"Looking like what?" I smirk.

"Don't pull that basic bitch act with me, you know exactly what I mean." She scowls. I chuckle loudly, thoroughly enjoying the look of displeasure on her face.

She hates how much she wants me, and watching her squirm is the best kind of fun.

She'll give in eventually; we both know it.

"You could come over here and join me?"

She prowls towards the bed, and for a second I think I'm about to become the luckiest bastard around.

She crawls onto the bed, straddles my hips and leans her face down, only an inch from mine, her hands pinning my wrists to the sheets.

"I could..." she purrs.

Jesus, the crazy shit this girl can do to me. I'm desperate for more. I thought she'd have given up, given in, but here I am, all set to become the one willing to beg.

"You know what you are?" she murmurs, her warm breath tickling my ear as she teases me, her hips grinding against me.

"*What*?" I reply, my voice unusually gruff.

"Too fucking easy." She sits up, smirks, and climbs off me.

What the hell?

"Jesus Christ, jailbait." I throw my head back.

I just got played, good and proper. I'm half hard, dying to feel her on top of me again, but I can't even be mad – she played me like a fiddle, and I have to respect her game.

She giggles and rolls her eyes at me. "Pathetic."

"Tease."

I rearrange myself and she watches, completed unashamed.

"You should take care of that." She tips her head towards my crotch.

"You offering?"

"That would be a *no*."

"You sure?"

"I'm no fortune teller, but I see a cold shower in your future."

I chuckle. "What's with all the decorations? Your mum already went crazy downstairs."

She smiles softly and it makes me smile too. "I just really like Christmas."

She stretches up on her tippy toes, trying to reach up to stick some hideous reindeer garland across her wall.

I jump off the bed, sidle up behind her and take it from her hand, pressing myself against her as I stick it up.

"What a gentleman," she drawls.

I press my crotch against her ass once more before backing off. "You can thank me later."

"Oh, I'll be sure to do that."

I pick up a Santa statue. "This thing is creepy. I don't know how you'd sleep with that watching you."

"Can you go play somewhere else? Surely there's a bunch of women waiting for you to take your clothes off somewhere?"

"Nope." I smirk. "Work doesn't start for a few hours yet."

"Lucky me," she mutters.

"I can practise on you, if you want?"

"Hard pass."

"You don't need to be embarrassed, it's okay to enjoy it."

She turns on me, her eyebrows raised and her expression one of absolutely no bullshit. "Out." She points at the door.

I try to do my best puppy-dog eyes, but given I've never begged a woman for a single thing in my life, I don't think I'm nailing it.

"Get. Out. Now." She shoves at my bicep, and I chuckle, letting her push me out of her bedroom.

I know damn well I'll be back. She'll see.

———

"THAT'S another level of hot. Seriously, if you don't bang that chick, I'm going to disown you."

I wipe the sweat off my chest and raise a brow at him. "When did you become so invested in me getting my dick wet?"

"I worry about you away at school, eyeballs deep in books. I'm just thinking about your balls, man."

"My balls are fine."

"They will be after you're finished with her."

He peers around the curtain again, and I catch sight of the smoking-hot redhead, sitting front and centre, a coy smile on her lips as she watches Helix doing his routine.

"If she's so hot, you take her upstairs."

"Can't, got plans."

"Maybe I've got plans too."

He huffs out a breath. "What? Like going home and messing around with Margot?"

I flip him off.

"Seriously, dude, I get it. She's hot as shit. Maybe even hotter than that chick giving you the bedroom eyes out there, but nothing is ever going to happen with you and the stepsister. She shot you down. Get over it."

Margot is at least ten times hotter than that chick, and given how mind-blowingly attractive that girl is, I figure I must be under some type of mind voodoo.

"Who have you got plans with?"

He shakes his head. "Nope, we're talking about you and your dick. Not mine."

"If I agree to go talk to that chick, will you tell me who you're meeting up with?"

I've got a pretty good feeling he's going to say Beth.

He's seen her once more since the night Margot and I hooked up, and now that I think about it, I haven't seen him pick up another chick lately.

He tips his head side to side, weighing up whether he's willing to make the deal.

"Fine, but only because I'm a good fucking wingman."

"If you say so."

"I'm meeting Ari."

My brows shoot up. "Who?"

"Just some chick I met. Now go talk to the girl."

He shoves me in the direction of the club, but I backtrack, calling him out. "You're bullshitting me, I can tell, your left eye is twitching."

"Fuck you."

"You're meeting Beth."

"Am not."

"Holy shit, you like that girl."

His eyes widen. "Do not."

Never met a guy as afraid of commitment as Griff. It's like he has a built-in radar for when having sex goes anywhere near relationship territory, and he gets off and runs in the opposite direction as fast as he can.

"She's a gymnast, LA. A. Gymnast. Do you know how flexible gymnasts are?"

"You admit you like her, and I'll have sex with that girl out there," I offer, knowing full well that he'll *never* go there.

He shoves me again, muttering under his breath. "Just go talk to her already."

I salute him as I chuckle. I might have found myself in a situation where I'm caught up in a woman just as much as he is, but it's always funnier when it's happening to someone else.

I slide past the curtain, making a beeline for the pretty redhead.

She really is drop-dead fucking gorgeous.

Her eyes find mine and her lips curl up into a grin.

Maybe this is exactly what I need. If Margot really wants nothing to do with me, there's other women who do.

10

Margot

THERE'S a loud bang in the hallway and my eyes fly open, my heart thumping in my chest.

"Ouch... *motherfucker*... who put that there?"

I rake my hands over my face.

Lukah.

I'm seriously surprised that Rick hasn't changed the locks to keep him out at this point.

I overheard a screaming match between the two of them the other night. Something about Lukah refusing to wear a shirt, and Rick threatening to call the police if he showed up pissed in the middle of the night again.

Clearly, Lukah heeded that warning.

I hear him stumbling down the hallway, swearing and cursing as he trips over something – probably his own feet.

"Fuck," his muffled voice says.

"Oh *come on*," I mutter to myself.

Rick and my mum will hear him if this carries on much longer, and then I'll have to endure Rick in a foul mood *and* watch my mother running around like a stupid woman, trying to cheer him up.

I slide out of bed and pad to the door, swinging it open at the same moment that Lukah must have leaned against it.

He falls into my room, landing heavily on the floor with a loud thud.

"Ow," he moans.

"For the love of god," I murmur as I kick his feet aside and shut the door quickly.

There's no way in hell I want him sleeping in here, but it's pretty fucking obvious he's not in any shape to make it to his own room without starting some type of fight with his dad... or breaking one of his legs.

"What the hell are you doing?" I grumble as I lean down, hooking my arms under his armpits in an attempt to sit him up.

"Being sneaky," he slurs, holding his finger up to his lips.

"Oh yeah, you're about as subtle as a freight train."

"Shhh," he mutters.

Christ. He's totally shit-faced.

"Can you get up?"

He half nods, half shakes his head.

Convincing.

"Your dad is going to flip if he finds out you came in wasted again."

He taps the end of my nose. "Boop." He chuckles, sloppy as hell.

"*Lukah*," I hiss.

"Who cares?" he drawls lazily, his head drooping. "I'm wearing a shirt."

He's right, I guess he followed one of the rules.

"I'm going to get you up on the bed, okay?"

He waggles his brows. "Now we're talking."

"We most certainly are not."

I pull hard and he does sweet fuck all to assist me with getting up to his feet, but we manage in the end, and he's on his feet, wobbling.

"You're really fucking hot," he says.

"Thank you," I reply as I try and get the button and zip undone on his jeans.

"See," he tries to help me and only ends up making it more difficult, "you just want to get me out of my pants."

"What can I say? Virtually unconscious men just do it for me," I deadpan sarcastically.

"I turned her down, you know?"

I get the button undone and the zip lowered as he leans his weight on me.

Stupid, heavy, drunk bastard.

"Who?"

"The chick from the club."

I shove the jeans down his legs, and he falls backwards onto the bed.

I sigh. He really isn't making this easy.

"She wanted the D... but I said no," he says, his tone indicating that he thinks it was a real achievement.

With some effort, I get his shoes off, and drag his jeans down his legs, throwing them in a pile on the floor.

"Well, I think she should count herself lucky."

He grunts, his eyes shut.

"I couldn't do it," he murmurs to himself.

"Are you going to move up to the pillows?"

He shakes his head, smiling. "Nope."

"Whatever." I shake my head and climb into bed, putting as much distance between us as the space will allow.

His head is at my stomach height, his long legs hanging over the end of the bed.

"She was hot too."

"Good for her."

"But..." he rolls over, facing me, eyes still shut, "she had nothing on you."

I still. *Did he...?*

"*What?*" I whisper.

"*Jailbait,*" he says, sleep thick in his tone.

"What did you say?" I try again, but I'm wasting my time. He's out like a light.

I groan.

He turned down a girl, *for me?*

I'd really like to get a few more hours sleep, but my mind is whirring.

Turning him down must really be fucking with his head, and his ego – that must be what this is. He's a man on a mission.

He starts snoring and I shove him. That achieves nothing, and I groan again.

"You better not pee the bed," I grumble as I cover my ears with my pillow.

––––––––

"Jailbait, wake up."

"Fuck off, five more minutes."

My shoulder shakes again. "Not happening, wake up."

I slowly open one eye and glare at him.

Asshole has the audacity to wake me up in the middle of the night, snore for hours on end, and then wake me up in the morning too.

It's a wonder I didn't stab him as he slept.

"There better be a fire, or I'm going to start plotting your death," I warn him.

I blink drowsily, my eyes adjusting and focusing on him. He's showered and changed.

"What time is it?" I grumble.

"Time for you to explain what the fuck happened to my bedroom."

A slow grin crosses my face. I actually forgot about that after his midnight antics.

"How are you so bright after being so wasted? Do you have some type of secret hangover recipe or something? Because I want details for future reference."

"Exercise and a green smoothie," he replies, not missing a beat, "but for real... What. The. Fuck?"

I snuggle back into my pillow. "I thought you might like some Christmas cheer."

"Well you thought wrong."

I bury a laugh.

"The creepy Santa? *Really*, Margot? That fucking thing just about gave me a heart attack when I went into my room."

"You're welcome."

"You can go and take all that crap out of there."

I roll over. "I'll do no such thing, and you're also welcome for getting your ass to bed last night before your dad got hold of you."

"We both know you'll do anything to get me into bed, jailbait." He winks.

I roll my eyes. "You're a real liability, you know that, right?"

He shrugs a shoulder.

"Seriously, you were drunk enough to still come onto me, but not in any way sober enough to actually do anything about it."

"I'm sober enough now."

Always with the innuendos.

I ignore his cheap attempt at flirting. "You weren't too drunk to tell me about the hotty from the club though."

His cocky expression shifts to one of surprise.

"That's right, hot shot, I know you want me so bad you can't get your dick up for anyone else."

"Vastly untrue."

"Liar."

"Demon."

"Limp dick."

We both burst into laughter.

"You know damn well that it's *anything* but." He points a finger at me.

I do know. I know really, *really* well. Too well. A massively unhealthy amount.

It would be so easy to find out again too. I could give in, *beg*. He wouldn't judge me, he'd just pleasure me.

I give myself a mental slap across the face.

Not happening.

I need to cleanse my thoughts with bleach or something. No amount of reason or logic seems to be doing the job. Not when it comes to Lukah.

He gets up off my bed and snags his pants and shoes from the floor. "Why'd you smuggle me in here anyway?"

Great question.

"Didn't really want to listen to you and Rick go

another round." I yawn. "Plus, you were about ten seconds away from breaking some ugly expensive piece of art out there."

It's the truth, but maybe, just maybe, a little part of me likes his company too – even when he's off his head.

"Well I appreciate it."

"And I'd appreciate it if you'd lay off the drink for a night or two."

"I'll see what I can do."

He heads for the door but stops short. "Seriously though, jailbait, you better help me get that shit out of my room, or I'm going to have a sacrificial burning of that Santa."

"That'll only wind you up on the naughty list."

He smirks, his boyish grin cocky as hell. "It's cute that you think I'd want to be anywhere else."

11

Lukah

"Get your jacket, I'm taking you out of this shit hole."

She doesn't even glance up at me, just flicks over another page of the magazine she's been reading for the past twenty minutes.

"I know you can hear me, jailbait."

"Kind of hard not to," she drawls, "you clearly like the sound of your own voice."

I grin. There she is. There's the wild child I've been missing.

"Seriously, get your shit."

"Seriously, stop talking." She mimics my tone.

"I need to go Christmas shopping."

"Not my problem."

"I need to get something for your mum."

That gets her attention, just like I knew it would, her eyes narrowing at me.

"You're playing dirty."

"Oh, babe, you know I get dirtier than this."

She rolls her eyes. "It's like six days until Christmas, town will be hellish."

"Don't have a choice, jailbait."

"But *I* do." She smirks, finally closing the stupid magazine and giving me her full attention.

We've been dancing around each other for days now. I haven't kissed her since the other night in the media room, but it's taking its toll on my self-control. We've been flirting in a way that's poorly disguised as fighting.

It's fucking exhilarating. It's like hate sex, just without the sex.

I thought she'd have cracked by now, but she's stronger willed than I anticipated, and that suits me just fine. The reward is always sweeter when you've had to work for it.

"I'll buy you something."

She raises a brow. "I'm listening."

"What do you want?"

"Depends what's on offer?"

"More than a chocolate milkshake, but less than diamond earrings." I chuckle.

She chews on her bottom lip as she considers it. "Alright fine. Let's go."

That was easier than I anticipated. I'll have to remember that a way to a woman's heart is sometimes through your credit card.

She gets up off her seat, grabs her bag and jacket from the stand near the door and swings it open. "*Wait*, do you even have a car?"

I usher her out and shut the door behind us. "Of course I have a car."

"Then why haven't I seen it in the garage?"

"Because my dad's a fuckwit and makes me park it on the street."

"You drive a piece of shit or something?" She grins.

"Do *you* think I'd drive a piece of shit?"

She rolls her eyes. "Probably not. Please don't tell me you drive a douchey convertible or something."

"No douchey convertible in sight." I chuckle as we hop into the elevator and begin the descent to the ground level.

"So, did you buy it in cash?" She smirks.

"Yeah, you should have seen the guy's face when I piled thirty grand's worth of fives on his desk."

"You *didn't*."

"Maybe I did."

The doors open and I guide her with my hand on the small of her back out into the lobby of the building and through the front door.

"So which one is yours?" She glances up and down the street.

I wish I'd bought my bike now, it would have been worth it to see the look on her face when I handed her a helmet and told her to climb on, not to mention the feeling of having her legs wrapped around me, but I guess having her in the front seat of my Chevy will have to do.

"This pretty little lady right here." I point to the classic car that should be inside, safe and dry.

She glances between me and the car, raising a brow as her eyes settle on me.

"What's the matter? Not what you expected?"

"Not even a little bit. You sure you're not messing with me?"

I jog around the front of the car and unlock the driver's door. "Get in, jailbait."

She tries the handle, but it's locked. Central locking is a bit beyond my baby. I lean over and unlock the door, and she slides in on the bench seat next to me.

"I gotta hand it to you, this is a sweet car." She runs her fingers across the dash, and she may as well be stroking *me*, because I feel my dick twitch in my jeans.

I clear my throat and start the engine.

She asks me a few questions about the car as we drive across town, but other than that, it's a comfortable silence between us.

I can't help but steal glances at her every few seconds. I might have been inside her, several times even, but somehow, her being in my car feels even more intimate.

I never pick up girls in my car. In fact, I never let girls anywhere near any of my private shit.

The club, bars... that's where I pick up chicks. It's usually one night and one night only. Out the back of the club, in the bathroom, or a hotel room. When I'm in town, I usually crash at Griff's.

I don't take girls back to my apartment, and I don't date – not anymore. So there's no driving back and forth to the movies or dinner or any of that bullshit.

It's just sex.

Plenty of women have caught my eye at school, but I'm not about to hook up after a lecture. Last thing I need is some hostile female staring daggers at me for the rest of the year after I don't call her back.

"So, what are you buying?" Margot asks, pulling my thoughts back to her and her sexy ass.

I shrug my shoulder. "No idea. That's why I brought you."

"Well who are you buying for, besides me, of course."

I get lucky with a park in the crowded carpark and kill the engine. She was right, this place looks crazy.

"Why aren't you at work or school or something?" I ask, ignoring the shopping question, because honestly, it was just an excuse to get her to go somewhere with me.

I turn on the seat to face her, my arm slung across the back of the bench.

"I took off two weeks for Christmas."

"Off from what?"

"I'm a hairdresser. I work over the other side of town."

"Why are you staying with my old man?"

A look crosses her features that I don't understand, but it's gone again before I can pry.

"My lease ran out and I haven't found a new place yet. It would have been a nightmare to try and find something over the holidays, so they said I could stay with them until the new year."

That was good of the old bastard. Pity he wouldn't extend the same invitation to his only child.

I nod. "Where's your boyfriend?"

She frowns at me. "What makes you think I have a boyfriend?"

"Saw the photo in your bedroom."

She's quiet in thought for a few seconds.

"*Hold up*, let me get this straight... you saw a photo in my bedroom, assumed I had a boyfriend, and then tried to kiss me anyway?"

"I didn't *try* to kiss you." I smirk. "I *did* kiss you."

"Even though you thought I was in a relationship?" she demands.

"I'd already fucked you for hours on end, Margot, do you really think I was about to draw the line at a kiss? And besides, I knew you weren't with the guy, you don't strike me as a cheating kind of girl."

Goosebumps form on her skin and she tugs on her sleeve to try and cover them.

"So you snoop at my photos, kiss me, then fish for information on a guy you didn't think was my boyfriend in the first place?"

"Something like that."

"Call me crazy, but you could have just asked who he was when you saw the picture." She shakes her head at me like she can't figure me out.

I can't figure me out either, can't figure out why I care about any of it, but I've asked now so I can't take it back.

"Who is he?"

"He's my ex."

"You keep his photo?"

"We're still friends."

"No one is really friends with their ex."

"Well *I* am. What would you know anyway? I bet you've never had a real relationship in your life. Lukah Andrews – serial playboy, what would you know?"

Apparently, I hit a nerve.

She reaches for the door handle and swings the door open before jumping out of the car and stomping in the direction of the elevators.

I've clearly said something to piss her off, but she's done the same to me.

I'm fucking tired of people assuming they know me because of something I do to make money. I take it from a lot of people in my life, but I'm *not* taking it from her.

I climb out of the car, slamming the door as I follow her, catching her quickly and tugging on her hand to halt her.

She fights against me, but I'm not having it. I pull hard, and she stumbles back towards me, her front colliding with mine.

"Don't throw that shit at me and then storm off like a brat."

She glares up at me. "I'm not a brat."

"Sure fucking look like one from where I'm standing." I grunt. "Only assholes make assumptions. Don't be an asshole."

"Oh, so it's fine for you to make assumptions about me, but not the other way around?"

"Fair point." I grunt. "Sorry."

Her expression softens.

"Thank you. And I'm sorry too, for calling you a playboy..."

I run a hand through my hair. I want this girl so bad; it's messing with my head. We made fireworks together and the damn things have blinded me... made me desperate to see them again.

"Do you know *why* I strip?"

She chews on her lip for a second, thinking. "Because you're hot?" she guesses.

I chuckle. "I appreciate the compliment, but it's for the money. For school."

She leans into me, just ever so slightly, and I figure, I'm already pushing my luck with her, I may as well take it one step further.

I snake my arm around her middle and pull her flush against me.

"For school?" she asks, confused, but not fighting my hold.

"I'm going to be a lawyer."

"Like, as in you're going to yell 'object' while taking your clothes off on stage?"

I chuckle. "No, as in, I'm a third-year law student."

Her jaw drops. "How did I not know that?"

"Because Rick doesn't know anything about it. I took some time off after high school to save enough money to pay for law school without having to ask my dad for a cent. He figured that stripping was my career choice and he's never asked me about it again."

"That's really sad."

"That's my dad for you."

"So, you stripped at that club from the other night?"

I nod. "Griff owns it, so he still lets me swing by when I'm in town and when I'm on break from school. Keeps my funds up."

"You don't strip where you live?"

I shake my head. "That's a different life for me out there. I'm going to be a lawyer before I know it, and I can't really combine the two."

She giggles. "Probably not if you want people to take you seriously."

"Exactly. Honestly, this trip back will probably be the last time, unless I fail my finals and don't pass the bar, and then I might have to go back to it."

"You won't fail," she says softly.

I release her wrist that I've been grasping and bring my hand up to cup her jaw. "Oh yeah, how can you be so sure?"

She swallows slowly. "Just got a good feeling about you."

"I've got a good feeling about you too," I murmur.

She's staring so intently into my eyes, it's making it

hard to remember that this is all fun and games, sex and banter.

I dip my head slowly and brush my lips softly against hers, in a kiss so sweet it's practically dripping in honey. She might not have begged, but I knew I was going to break that rule the moment I made it.

I pull back and her eyes stay closed a moment before slowly flitting open.

She's so fucking beautiful, so sexy, so god damn forbidden.

My heart is racing, and I hate it. That's not what *this* is. I don't want any part of me reacting to her, unless it's the part between my legs.

I clear my throat. "C'mon. Let's go spend my dirty stripper money."

12

Margot

"Go-go, did I just see you and Lukah come in together?" Mum asks as she strolls into my room, her eyes scanning over the numerous shopping bags on my bed.

I knew damn well that Lukah didn't intend to do fuck all Christmas shopping, but there were sales on, so I made him carry my bags while he bitched and moaned about being treated like a boyfriend with none of the boyfriend perks.

He did buy some soap for my mum, so there's that at least. I suggested he get something for his dad, but he told me that hell wasn't freezing over just yet.

"Yeah, he needed some help Christmas shopping..."

"You two seem to be getting along well."

I raise a brow at her. I'm pretty confident that we spend more time hurling insults at one another than we do getting along, but I know what she means. My mum is a perceptive woman, there's not much that gets by her – my ongoing flirtation with Lukah included apparently.

"I've seen the way he's been looking at you, go-go."

Mum has called me 'go-go' since I was about three years old.

I busy myself with the bags. "Mmm, how's that?"

"Like he wants to rip your clothes off and screw you up against a wall."

"Mum!" I gape at her.

"Oh please, I'm not a hundred. I'm aware there is sex outside of the missionary position."

Jesus Christ.

"Well... that's... good to know."

"Seriously, Margot, I think you should stay away from him. He's trouble."

He's trouble alright, with a capital fucking 'T', but she's wasting her breath – I'm not about to run off into the sunset with the guy.

There's an attraction between us, and that's it. I want nothing more from Lukah than his hard dick, and even that, I'm resisting for the greater good.

"You've got nothing to worry about, Mum. We're just giving each other a hard time."

She nods, the look in her eyes disbelieving, and reaches out to take the new top I'm holding.

I pass it to her, and she holds it up. "Cute."

"Do you know why Lukah and Rick give each other such a hard time?" I pry, hoping that she has some information that could help me understand what went on between the two men to make them despise even being in the same room together.

She frowns. "I'm not sure exactly. Rick said they had a falling out years ago. I think it might have been when Rick and Lukah's mum split up. Maybe Lukah didn't take it too well?"

I shrug my shoulders. Maybe that's all it is. A messy divorce could have been what it took to pit father against son.

"I'm going to meet Miranda for dinner tonight, do you want to come with?"

I shake my head. I'm beat. I just want to put on my PJ's and curl up with some Netflix and popcorn. If I go out with Mum and Miranda, we'll end up drinking cocktails and that could lead to anything.

I'm not up for a repeat of one of those nights. I need some peace and quiet.

Lukah is hitting the strip club tonight, so I know he won't be bothering me. Maybe I'll even be able to relax. But just the thought of him taking his clothes off has the opposite reaction to relaxing, so maybe not.

"I'll pass... say hi to her from me though."

She drops the top on my bed, leans in and kisses my forehead. "Will do. I can leave you some pizza money if you want?"

I huff out a laugh. "I'm twenty-three, I think I can pay for my own pizza."

"I know." She grins. "But didn't you hear? I'm rich now."

I laugh loudly. "Mum! That's terrible."

"It's true though." She giggles as she leaves the room.

I rummage through the bags until I find the pair of skin-tight black jeans that I made Lukah buy for me as payment for going with him into town.

They're sexy as hell. I know when I look good wearing a pair of jeans, and I look damn good in these.

I smirk as I think about him dropping actual cash to

buy them. The store attendant thought we were crazy, laughing and joking about what he has to do to earn that much money.

I tried to drag him into a jewellery store to look at a small oval locket I saw in the window, but he flat-out refused to buy me anything shiny.

Told me it was boyfriend bullshit that he wanted no part of.

He was right, the last thing I'd want is to think about him every time I put the thing on anyway, but it sure was pretty.

I throw all the shit I got on the chair in the corner and go take a shower.

I can't help but think about Lukah as the hot water pelts my skin. This might not be the shower wall he pressed me up against, but it may as well be for how vividly my memories are coming back to me.

I'd had a fair bit to drink that night, and I'd like to blame the alcohol for the way I behaved with Lukah, but he was right, I wasn't *that* drunk.

I remember every single detail about how it felt to be with him.

Part of me wishes things were different between us, that I didn't dislike him and lust after him in equal parts, but that's the reality. He drives me insane in more ways than one.

He's my stepbrother, he's a ladies' man, and above all that, he's just *not* the one for me.

I come out of the bathroom wearing nothing but a towel and shriek as the figure in front of me gives me a huge fright.

"Jesus, Rick." I clutch at the top of the towel. "You scared the shit out of me."

He holds up his hands in apology. "Sorry, honest mistake."

I tug the towel higher, feeling self-conscious as I feel his eyes on me.

There's something about Rick; it's like he can be looking at you without directly staring. He's quick, perhaps a little sly. I never noticed it before, but since the other night when he came into my room, I've been more aware of him.

"Do you know where your mum is?"

I breathe out a sigh of relief. He's looking for my mum. I've got to stop overreacting about our every interaction.

"She went out for dinner with Miranda. I guess she'll be back later on…"

He nods. "Right, I think she told me that."

"Don't tell me you're already turning into a husband who has selective hearing," I joke, trying to settle the feeling of unease in my belly.

He grins. "Don't tell your mother."

I smile and shift my weight from one foot to the other. I'd feel a lot more comfortable having this conversation if I wasn't naked under my towel.

"What about *Lukah*? Where's he?"

He can't even say his son's name without it coming out bitter.

"Work," I reply quietly, realising in that moment that I'm on my own with him.

It shouldn't be a problem, but right now it's starting to feel like one.

His eyes meet mine, blue, just like Lukah's.

He takes a step forward, and the scent of alcohol wafts towards me.

"So, we're all alone then," he says, his mind connecting the dots the same way mine has.

Chills race down my spine and this time I don't think I'm overreacting at all.

That comment was suggestive. I *can't* be imagining it.

"Yeah, um... I guess. I was going to order a pizza and watch a movie... I don't know what's on Netflix, but I'll find something," I ramble, trying and failing to dissolve the uncomfortable feeling in the air around me.

He nods, still unmoving.

I could get past him if I wanted to, but I'll have to brush up against him, and a little voice in my head tells me that that's exactly what he wants me to do.

"I might go get dressed."

He holds his hand out, gesturing for me to go ahead whilst still not shifting his position.

I swallow deeply.

Is this really happening? Is my mum's brand-new husband subtly hitting on me, or is this some attempt to get me out of the way...? Maybe he wants me to move out sooner rather than later and thinks that making me uncomfortable will do it.

If that's his mission, then it's fucking accomplished. I want to pack my bags and get the hell out of here. Right now.

He still hasn't moved, and his eyes are challenging me.

"Excuse me," I say.

He takes one tiny step sideways, the corners of his mouth twitching with a grin.

He's enjoying this.

Bastard.

Tears threaten to spill from my eyes, but I won't let him see how much this is scaring me.

I rush forward, trying to get past him without making contact and failing.

His chuckle follows me down the hall as I walk as fast as I can, my heart pounding more violently with every step I take.

I glance back over my shoulder, but he's not there anymore.

My bedroom has a lock on the door, but it doesn't feel like enough. I can't stay here. I'll have to call Beth – see if I can stay the night with her.

I spin back around and collide with a broad chest.

"Woah, jailbait." Lukah reaches out to steady my shoulders. "Where's the fire?"

Oh there's a fire alright, and I feel like I was seconds away from getting burnt.

I check over my shoulder again, before trying to skirt around him, but he's not having it, his grip on my shoulders tightening.

I thought he was gone, and as grateful as I am in this second not to be alone with Rick, I'm also horrified at the idea of Lukah seeing me like this.

"Margot, what's wrong? You're shaking."

I bring my hand up to my face. He's right. My entire arm is trembling.

"I... your dad... I just... I want to get dressed."

His face turns to stone. "What did he do?" he demands.

I've never heard his voice sound so cold.

"Nothing," I whisper. "He didn't do anything."

"He must have fucking done *something* for you to be freaking out like this." He dips his head so we're at eye level to one another. "Tell me, jailbait."

"I just felt uncomfortable," I reply quietly.

"What. Did. He. Do?"

"I think he hit on me," I breathe.

He's pushing past me in a second, anger radiating from him.

"Lukah, no." I grab his arm and tug him back.

"I'm going to fucking kill him." He tries to shrug me off.

"No," I plead with him, "please don't. Please don't leave me."

He stills, slowly meeting my eyes over his shoulder.

I don't know how my face looks, but if it's anything like the way I feel, it's not pretty.

"I don't want you to leave me."

He inhales deeply through his nose, and then out through his mouth, calming himself with each deep breath.

He checks his watch and then points at my bedroom door. "Get dressed. Pack a bag. You're coming with me."

Much like when he told me to wait for him after his strip show, I do exactly what I'm told.

13

———

Lukah

Bright fucking red.

That's all I can see.

Rage. Pure fucking rage is festering in the pit of my stomach, just begging to be let loose.

If it weren't for the fact that Margot had pleaded with me, I would have given my old man what he's had coming for the past however many god damn years.

I grip the steering wheel in my fists, my knuckles turning white as I picture the terrified look in her eyes.

Margot has sat next to me in silence for the entire drive so far, not saying a damn word, but she's got her packed bag on the seat next to her, so that's one positive in this colossal fuck-up of a situation.

She didn't even ask where I'd be taking her. Just packed her shit, put her trust in me and got in the car.

It's a scary fucking thing, having someone's trust given

to you so easily. It's something I'm bound to screw up. Just like my dad did this evening. Not that I'd *ever* pull the tricks he does.

"Did he touch you?" I demand, the question coming out harsh and aggressive.

She shakes her head quickly. "I think he was just trying to make me feel uncomfortable."

She's got no fucking idea what he was probably trying to do.

He's a creep through and through, and the sooner Margot, *and* Kate figure that out – the better off they'll be.

It took wife number two a couple of years to come to her senses, but she did eventually, Kate can too.

"Tell me. *All of it*. From the beginning."

"I came out of the bathroom and he was just there," she whispers.

Came out, wearing nothing but a towel, *vulnerable*. That prick intimidated her half-naked.

"He didn't touch me. He didn't even really say anything. I'm probably making a big deal out of nothing... but it was his vibe... he thought we were alone, and he knew he was frightening me."

"I don't *ever* want you alone with him again," I insist gruffly, as though I have the right to tell her what to do.

"Okay," she replies.

I slam my hand down on the dash and mutter a string of profanities under my breath.

I should have fucking stayed away. I never should have gone to his apartment that night. I should have stayed at Griff's. If I'd done that, I'd be back home by now, and none of this would be my problem.

But she's here now, in my mind and in my life, and as long as *she's* here, then it's most definitely my problem.

"He'd been drinking," she says after giving me some time to calm myself down. "I'm sure he'll feel like an asshole in the morning."

"He needs to feel like an asshole for the rest of his life, but that's the thing about Rick. He never does," I growl. "And you know what? Even if he did, it still wouldn't be enough for making you feel like that."

She's about to ask me another question, but I'm just pulling into the carpark of the strip club.

"We'll finish this later," I tell her. "I'm late."

"I don't really feel like watching the show tonight."

"You can hang out on the couches out back or go up to Griff's apartment and watch TV or whatever you want, but there is no way in hell that you're going anywhere else without me, understood?"

She nods slowly.

I can see she's still shaken. Fucking don't blame her.

My dad is a grade-A prick.

I kill the engine, grab my bag and jump out of the car.

She's still sitting inside when I round the front and pull her door open.

She looks up at me with wide eyes, and shit, maybe I'm a prick too because all I can think about doing is throwing her over my shoulder, carrying her upstairs and picking up where we left off the other night.

But I can't do that, not yet. I'm all she's got right now, and if she can't trust me, then she's fucked.

I hold out my hand to help her up, and she takes it.

"Thank you, for this," she says as I lead her towards the back door, her hand still in mine.

This is probably the longest we've ever gone in each other's company without either insulting one another or getting it on.

"Don't thank me for not being a douche like my dad."

"I'm not. I'm thanking you for taking care of me."

I clear my throat. I'm not much of a nurturer, and suddenly I feel like a fraud.

I'm not some hero with the rights or the skill set to take care of *anyone*. I barely take care of myself, but I didn't have a choice. Not this time.

I stride ahead, dragging her along, when she speaks. "You're nothing like him, you know?"

I know I'm not. Never fucking will be, but the way she's been treating me, like she doesn't want to get too close, she could have fooled me.

I've got her backed up against the grotty brick wall out back in a flash, my arms caging her in.

She gasps, but there's none of the fear she had in her eyes earlier. No, there's nothing but want.

I run my nose up the column of her throat and across to her ear, before dragging the lobe between my teeth.

"Are you sure about that?"

She shivers, nodding her head. "I'm sure."

"Maybe I'm the kind of guy who takes what he wants too?"

"There's a difference," she breathes as I kiss down her jaw.

"And what's that?" I murmur.

Our gaze locks and I see her warring with herself.

"The *difference...* is, as much as I hate myself for it... I want to give *you* what you want."

———

"DUDE," Griff says, a massive grin on his stupid face.

"Don't say it," I growl.

"*Dude*," he repeats, laughing.

"Fuck off, Griff, I swear to god."

"You brought a chick. To the club. A *chick*. To. The. Club."

Fucking bastard is grinning from ear to ear.

"We're spose to pick them up here, man, not bring them along at the start."

I ignore him as I work my way through another set of push-ups.

"I never thought I'd see the day; eternal bachelor, Lukah Andrews, bringing his chick to the club."

"She's not *my* chick."

"Good point. She's your sister. *Sister fu–*"

"What was your cousin's name again?" I cut him off.

He chuckles. "I don't know what you're talking about."

I roll over and smash out some sit-ups.

"Just leave it, Griff, for real, I'm not in the fucking mood."

"Well bad luck, buttercup, leaving things alone isn't one of my strengths."

Don't I fucking know it.

"Tell me why you brought her, and I'll lay off."

"Blow me."

"I'd have to charge you."

I lie down on the floor, closing my eyes before I do something stupid, like knockout my best mate.

"I had no choice." I sigh, glaring at him. "If her being here is a big deal, I'll sort something else out."

"Had no choice, *why*?" he pries, still grinning. He's enjoying this way too fucking much.

As per fucking usual. Being a menace is his real talent.

"My dad was creeping on her, okay? You fucking happy now? Her mum is out, and he scared the living shit out of her back at home. There was no way in hell I was leaving her there alone with him."

His grin drops, and his eyes turn hard. "You serious?"

"Yeah, I'm fucking serious," I growl as I jump to my feet. "He didn't touch her; if he had, you'd probably be bailing me out down at the station."

He runs his hand through his hair. "I really fucking hate your dad."

"You and me both," I mutter.

"We should go over there and teach him a lesson."

Griff is *always* ready to throw down. He's a pain, but he's got my back, always, no questions asked. Well actually, usually one thousand questions asked, but never one single objection.

He claps me on the shoulder. "You did the right thing, bringing her."

I drag my hands down my face. "If it's a problem, I can book her a hotel room or some–"

"It's not a problem. *At all.* I was just giving you shit about falling for a girl. She's welcome anytime. She's out back sorting props for the guys. They're loving it."

"I'm not falling for her."

"You keep telling yourself that."

I want to argue further, but honestly, I haven't got the energy to deny shit that is really starting to feel real.

"But for real, bro, if you don't want to lose her to Helix, you might want to get back there. He's turning on the charm."

"She's too smart to fall for Helix's bullshit." I chuckle, relaxing.

"Wouldn't be so sure, LA, she fell for yours."

The smart little prick ducks out of the way as I reach out to slug him.

I get him in a headlock and wrestle him out the back where I find a smiling Margot, surrounded by the boys.

She's laughing and covering her eyes as Helix shows off, gyrating his hips in front of her.

I push Griff ahead and hang back to watch her.

She needs a good laugh after tonight. No matter how bad the urge to drag Helix away from her might be.

He turns, giving her a view of his ass in his ridiculous yellow g.

"*LA*." He grins, catching sight of me,."I was just showing Margot how it's really done."

I raise a brow at him. "Get any closer to her and I'll be showing *you* a couple of things."

He chuckles. "Told you," he calls out to Conrad, "pay up."

Conrad scowls, crosses the room and slaps a hundred into Helix's waiting palm.

I don't even ask. Something tells me the answer would only make me want to bolt.

"Seriously, can you put some pants on or something?" Margot giggles.

Helix winks at me, and strolls away, one hundred dollars and one warning richer.

"You good?" I ask as I close the distance between me and Margot and drop to a crouch in front of her.

She nods. "I can't believe I'm saying it, but I needed this. Thank you for bringing me here with you."

She reaches out, her palm gently cupping my jaw before leaning in and pressing a kiss to my cheek.

"You're welcome," I reply, tone gruff.

Fuck. Griff was right. This isn't just messing around – not for me.

"Hate to break up this little love fest, but you're on in two minutes, Romeo," Griff tells me.

Margot flips him off, saving me a job and I chuckle.

"I better go."

"Have fun out there." She smirks.

"You're not coming to watch?"

She shakes her head. "We both know what happened the last time I did that."

"We sure do. Why do you think I offered?"

She rolls her eyes and shoves me away, a blinding grin on her face.

"Pig."

"Holdout."

"Show pony," she throws back as I head for the stage.

There she is, my wild child.

14

Margot

Jesus.

I shouldn't have looked, but *as if* that was ever going to happen. I'm only human after all.

There are hot dudes out there. *Hot*, half-naked dudes.

One in particular, *obviously*, has my full attention, as much as I hate to admit it.

He's too good at what he does. He'd better be one hell of a lawyer, or it'll be a dire waste of a life.

I watch as he drops himself into the lap of some chick sitting up the front, near the stage.

She's yelling and cheering, and he's giving it to her, but there's no spark, no eye contact, no chemistry.

Nothing like what we shared in this same room.

He's just doing a job today, nothing more.

One thing is for sure though, he's making it really hard

for me to remember why I said no to a repeat performance.

I don't want to think about it, but it's there in my brain, screaming away, desperately trying to be heard.

I want him.

I want him *bad*.

My stepbrother.

My fantasy come to life.

My god damn weakness.

"Shit," I mutter under my breath.

This wasn't part of the plan. *He* wasn't part of the plan. Sex with no strings has never been more complicated.

"He's going soft, you know that, right?"

I spin around, clutching my chest in fright. "Wha... *what*?"

Griffin smirks at me, inclining his head out towards where Lukah is doing his thing. "My boy. He's going soft."

I'm fairly fucking certain there's *nothing* soft about Lukah Andrews, but I'm not really willing to get into that with Griff right now. It won't help my case in the least.

"Never seen him like this," he continues.

"Like what?" I pull my eyes off the gorgeous man that's taking up far more space in my head than I'd like to admit.

"This into a chick. *You*."

"It's just physical."

"No denying that's part of it, but that's not all there is to it. He told me what happened tonight."

I feel my cheeks heat. "He did?"

I have nothing to be embarrassed about, but I am regardless. The whole thing is humiliating.

"Haven't seen a look in his eye like that in..." he pauses, "in a *long* time." He finishes. "He's protective of you, and he only protects something if he feels pretty fucking strongly about it."

I shrug a shoulder. "Maybe he feels like he has to look out for me, like a little sister."

I know it's nonsense the minute it leaves my lips, but I'm desperately clutching at straws here.

Griff bursts into laughter. "Look, I give LA a hard time about being a sister fucker and all that, but you two *aren't* family. You're together because of circumstance, but there's absolutely no obligation for him to take care of you – he's doing that because he wants to."

I don't think I believe any of this. Griff is wrong, has to be.

It's about sex. Plain and simple.

We were good together, hottest sex of my life, *hands down*... and then I pulled the brakes.

Lukah is the kind of guy who likes a challenge – the chase. He only wants me so bad because I've said no.

Not that I care, after Christmas comes and goes, we'll go our separate ways and probably cross paths once a year, max.

We're not destined to be in each other's lives and I'm good with that. That's what I have to keep telling myself anyway.

There might be more to Lukah than taking his clothes off for money and having sex with anything with a pulse, but he *is* that guy, just a little bit. Whether he wants to admit it or not.

Lukah jumps back up on the stage, catching my attention and our eyes lock firm.

He smirks, that stupid, cocky smirk of his and I shake my head in amusement.

I'm in a whole world of trouble here.

He looks too good, too tempting... too enticing.

I don't have the will power to deny it any longer.

He prowls towards me, seeing nothing but me.

I don't know, or care, if Griff is still hanging around, but if he is, I have a feeling he's about to get a show.

"You watched," Lukah says as he pushes past the curtain and stops, toe to toe with me.

"I caught a few seconds," I reply, nonchalant.

He hoists me up, lifting my ass onto a crate and sliding himself between my legs, stealing the breath right out of my lungs.

"Deviant." He smirks, fingers digging into my thighs.

"Egocentric."

My hands in his hair.

"Frigid."

His mouth on my skin.

"Tool."

My legs around his waist.

"Fucking *mine*," he growls, and then we're moving, our chests pressed together, my thighs locked tight around his waist.

"Please," I beg, giving him what I know he wants.

I hope he didn't have another dance scheduled for tonight, because if that's the case, he's about to leave Griff real high and dry.

We make it halfway up the stairs before he stops and slams me roughly against the wall.

"Jerk." I grunt.

"Whinge."

"Narcissist."

"Hellcat."

"You fucking know it." I smirk.

A deep rumble comes from somewhere deep inside him and then his lips are on mine, his tongue in my mouth, his hips grinding into me until we both run out of breath.

"You make me crazy, jailbait," he says, his voice raw as he leans his forehead against mine, his hips pressing me against the wall painfully.

"You're going to get me in *so* much trouble."

"Look around," he growls as he nips at my neck, "we're already in trouble."

So much god damn trouble. The kind of trouble I never saw coming.

He pulls back, those blue eyes staring right at me. "You up for a little trouble?"

"One last time," I breathe.

He shakes his head. "No deal, just let go, jailbait."

No more than five minutes ago, he was giving some other chick a lap dance, that alone should be enough to make me run a mile, but for some reason, I can't.

He's the brightest red flag I've ever seen, and I must be a complete idiot, because I don't run. I *don't* say no. In fact, all I do is nod.

———

HE PULLS ME CLOSER, our chests heaving as he wraps me tightly in his arms.

"What's with the death grip?"

"If you're going to try run again, I'm going to make it hard for you," he growls.

I huff out a laugh. "You're just going to hold me hostage?"

I don't know how the fuck he does that, but one flick of his legs between mine, and I'm on my back, my hands pinned above my head and his weight pressing deliciously into me.

"Something tells me you might enjoy that too much."

"You're insatiable."

"Only when it comes to you," he says, his reply muffled as he nuzzles my neck, the fingers on his free hand skimming up and down my skin, making my back arch off the bed.

"What are we doing?" I moan as he explores lower, tugging one of my nipples into his mouth and sucking.

"I'm pretty sure you know the answer to that."

"That's not what I mean."

He nips at my skin once more before sliding back up my body to look at me.

He releases my hands and rests his weight on his elbows.

My fingers find their way into his dirty-blond hair of their own accord, running through the strands.

I pull, bringing his lips to mine, kissing him until I'm desperately hungry for more.

"Does it matter what we're doing? Can't we just do what we want and say fuck you to the rest of it?" he asks, his eyes almost pleading with me.

"I don't think we can."

"Why not?"

"My mum, for one. Your dad for two," I reply, shuddering when I think about his father.

"I don't give a fuck," he growls. "Not about him."

"Doesn't change the fact that we're family now."

"Still don't give a fuck."

I'm not sure I do either. I can't think straight, not after

he just tipped my whole world upside down. Something that feels that good can't possibly be wrong.

"I'm not giving this up, not for him."

I try not to think too hard about what 'this' is.

"What's the deal between you guys? Why do you hate him so much?"

"He's not a good man, jailbait, the further away you stay from him, the better, trust me on that."

I nod. That's all I'm going to get out of him, I can tell.

"What's the deal with your dad?" he asks, turning it back on me.

I shrug. "Wouldn't know. Never met the guy. He and my mum were only casual, and he had no desire to be a dad, so he left when she found out she was pregnant with me. Never came back."

"What a fucking pair we are," he grumbles. "It's a wonder we haven't got daddy issues."

"You've definitely got some type of issues," I tease.

He bites my shoulder.

"Ouch!"

He chuckles, his grin cheeky.

"What about your mum? Where's she?" I've wondered about his mum, but never had the chance to ask.

"She travels all over for work, doesn't really have anywhere she calls home, but she comes by and visits me a few times a year. We talk on the phone a bit. She's a good woman, but she never really recovered from breaking up with Rick. She's never had another relationship, never really settled down... maybe one day she will."

"That makes me sad."

He kisses my forehead. "Nah, don't feel too bad about it, she's got a pretty awesome son."

I roll my eyes. "Rate yourself."

"She'd like you."

That's really sweet of him to say.

"I'm sure I'd like her too."

"She'd make a much better impression than fucking Rick."

I think a steaming pile of dog shit would make a better impression than he has been.

"Fuck him," I mutter.

"Fuck him," he agrees. "He's nothing."

"So... you think we should just keep using each other for sex?" I ask.

"We're not using each other; we're having fun."

We're one hundred percent using one another, but he can think what he wants about it.

I don't even know why I'm entertaining the idea of this, but I know one thing, I can't go back to the way things were... him tempting me every minute of the day, dangling himself in front of me like a carrot.

I might act strong, but my will power is virtually non-existent when it comes to this man.

"If we're going to do this, it has to be our secret," I bargain.

"You embarrassed of me, jailbait?"

"Embarrassed about fucking my stepbrother? You bet your ass I am."

He chuckles. "Don't worry, history suggests my dad won't be able to hold onto your mum for long anyway. I doubt we'll be stepsiblings for long."

"Whatever. I still won't like you."

"If that's what you need to tell yourself." He smirks, calling me on my lie.

I roll my eyes. "Douchebag."

"Spitfire."

"Twat."

"Vixen."

I don't get to retaliate, he silences me the best way he knows how, with his mouth on mine and his hard length pressing firmly between my legs.

15

Lukah

I PIN her against the wall as I pass her in the hallway, a gasp leaving her pretty, pouty lips.

"Do you think anyone would notice if I fucked you right here?" I growl in her ear.

"*Lukah*," she moans, and *god* the way she says my name gets me so hard, *instantly*. It's like a secret switch that only she has been able to find.

I snuck into her room just last night, but it's not enough. I'm more than ready to go again.

"You'd like that, wouldn't you, dirty girl?"

"I might."

I hear my dad thumping his way down the stairs and I drag Margot's ear lobe into my mouth, grazing her sensitive skin with my teeth before stepping back at the last second, leaving her wanting more.

"Tease," she whispers across the hall.

"Diva," I whisper back.

"Morning," my dad barks, and I turn away from him without a word.

I want nothing more than to deck him square in the nose, but I made Margot a promise.

She catches my eye and gives her head a subtle shake.

I might be a good for nothing stripper in the eyes of my father, but she makes me want to prove him wrong, so I keep my fists clenched at my sides.

"Morning, Rick," she replies to my piece-of-shit, good-for-nothing dad.

I don't know how she does it – pretends nothing happened between them.

I see the tense of her muscles, the hardness in her eyes and hear the edge to her voice, but to someone who hadn't studied her as closely as I have, you wouldn't think anything was amiss.

I know she's trying to give him the benefit of the doubt, trying to protect her mum, and attempting to keep me calm, but something is bound to give at some point.

He passes us, not even sparing me a second glance.

"I should break his fucking nose," I growl, closing the space between us once more. I'm wound so tightly, I could go after him in a flash, but being close to her stops me. I crave contact with her more than I want to feel my fists hitting his flesh.

"I should let you." She caresses my jaw softly, drawing my focus back to her.

"Say the word, jailbait," I promise her, "I won't need to be told twice."

Her dark eyes soften, and she presses a kiss to the corner of my mouth. "Thank you."

"Thank me *after* I punch him."

She giggles. "It's Christmas. You can't punch people at Christmas."

"Then I'll wait until New Year's." I smirk.

"You'll be back to your fancy law school by then," she replies, and maybe I'm imagining it, but I swear I hear a hint of disappointment in her tone.

Wishful thinking and all that.

"Go out with me today."

Her brows lift. "Like a date?"

"Like two people going out to eat."

She mulls it over. I can practically hear her thoughts running through her mind.

"I can't," she finally answers.

"Bullshit."

"Excuse me?"

"I said bullshit. There's no such thing as can't. You *won't*."

"Don't psychoanalyse me," she replies, sassy as shit. "I *can't*, because Beth is coming over to hang out, thank you very much."

"Beth, the chick who hooked up with Griff?" I smirk.

She nods. "The very one."

"Perfect." I chuckle. "We'll swing by and get him on the way too then."

"*What*?"

"Double date, jailbait."

Her lips curve up. "I thought we were just two people going out to eat."

Fucking technicality.

"Well now we'll be *four* people."

She grins, biting her lip.

"Why do I feel like I don't have a choice?"

I smirk. "Because you *don't*. Don't even pretend that you're going to say no; you're dying to say yes to me."

"Cocky much?"

"I'm as cocky as you are predictable."

"Don't act like you know me."

"I know you better than you think, jailbait."

I step into her body, pressing her against the wall again as my hands trail up her sides, making her shiver.

There's a knock at the door, but my eyes don't leave hers, not for a second.

"What's it going to be?" I murmur as I kiss her neck, her jaw, her throat, my fingers skating across the soft skin underneath her shirt.

"I guess I could eat," she pants. So damn needy.

"So could I."

"No sense in going separately," she replies, breathless as I continue teasing her.

There's another knock at the door as I drag my thumbs over the lace of her bra.

"You'd better get that, jailbait."

She catches me off guard, leaning in and pulling my bottom lip between her teeth.

I moan.

There's something so fucking hot about doing this with her out here where we could be caught at any second.

"I'll go, but *you're* paying," she whispers before shifting around me and skipping off to get the door.

I chuckle, shaking my head as I rearrange myself in my jeans.

My wild child, she's going to be the death of me.

———

"DUDE, I NEED COFFEE," Griff moans.

I dragged his hungover ass out of bed after Margot and Beth were ready to go, and he's been whining like a little bitch ever since.

"Calm your tits, man, we'll be there in a minute."

"Calm *my* tits? *You* woke me up early."

"It's after eleven." I chuckle. "Unless you're a fucking vampire, it's not early."

"It's a tough gig, that stripper life," Margot teases. "Up all night. Asleep all day... having to get your balls waxed..."

Griff isn't the only one who's up all night at the moment, I am too... in more ways than one.

I glance at Griff in the rear-view mirror, a smirk on my lips.

He flips me off.

Beth leans across and whispers something in his ear.

Fuck knows what she said, I'm not sure I even want to know, but he perks right up, grinning to himself, so I'd be willing to bet it's got something to do with his dick. It's the only thing he knows how to think with.

"Where we headed, trouble?" Margot asks me, almost bouncing in her seat.

If I'd known that double dates got her so excited, I would have asked a week ago.

"Out of town," I reply.

I'm more of a restaurant guy than I am a picnic one, but with two days to go until Christmas, even I'm not brave enough to try and get a table somewhere.

Instead, I swung by the store and loaded up with supplies.

"*Mysterious.*" She smirks.

I reach across the bench seat and tuck her palm in mine.

I don't know how she'll react to that. I half expect her to dig her nails into my hand or something, maybe scratch my eyes out, but she just stares at our intertwined hands for a few beats, and then glances out the window.

We haven't talked about hiding our relationship – or whatever this is – from our mates, so I'm testing the boundaries, seeing what she will and won't allow, because I know one thing, it's going to be a real long day if I can't touch her the way I want to.

I tighten my grip, and she looks back at me, deciding.

I virtually see the 'fuck it' cross her features.

She slides across the seat, sidling right up next to me, and tilts her face up to kiss my jaw.

Guess that answers that.

"Awwww," Beth says. "You two are *finally* a thing."

"Yeah, boy!" Griff whoops.

I chuckle as I sling my arm around Margot's shoulder.

She giggles, covering her face with her hands as their teasing cat calls continue.

My heart is thumping in my chest, this is so unlike me – fucking elated because a chick decided to claim me.

I'm usually the guy keeping women on the down low, sending them on the walk of shame, not letting them linger in my bed, let alone in my head.

But Margot... she's *different*. I don't know what the fuck that means, but for now, I'm content not to think too hard about it.

I kiss the top of her head, her springy curls tickling my nose and her sexy scent filling my head.

I pull up to the park and kill the engine. There's hardly anyone around, and that suits me.

I climb out and reach back in the car to help Margot out the driver's side after me.

I slam the door and then she's pressed up against it in the next breath.

"You know how fucking sexy it is when you stake your claim?"

"I'm not claiming anything," she replies, always fucking arguing with me. "Don't let your ego get in the way of the truth."

I grin. I love this game.

"You're such a bitch."

"And you love me." She smirks.

Maybe I do.

I balk, totally caught off guard by the unwelcome thought.

She doesn't notice, slipping around me to follow Griff, who's making a beeline for a coffee cart a few hundred metres away, Beth going with her.

"I guess I'll get the stuff," I call after them.

Margot turns, walking backwards as she smirks at me. "Put those muscles you're always flexing to good use."

"You make me sound shallow, jailbait."

"You said it, not me."

"Savage," I yell after her.

"Tool," she replies.

"Bimbo."

"Airhead," she fires back, grinning like crazy as the distance between us grows.

"You two are so fucking weird," I hear Beth say.

I chuckle, pop the boot and start putting my muscles to use.

16

Margot

"WHAT ARE you going to do when he leaves to go back home?"

I throw another handful of ripped-up bread into the lake and watch as the hordes of ducks all dive for it.

"What do you mean?"

She frowns at me. "He's not staying, you know that, right? He'll be gone again soon."

"And?" I prompt.

"And then what? Are you going to go with him?"

I frown at her. "Why on earth would I go with him?"

She gives me an 'oh please' look. "Girl, don't bullshit me, you're crazy about the guy."

He makes me crazy alright, but not in the way she's thinking.

"I think you've got the wrong impression."

She rolls her eyes. "Yeah, because there's *so* many ways

to misinterpret the way you two are together. You're all over each other."

"I'm not saying we're not, but haven't you ever had sex without feelings?"

"Just with the one guy." She sighs wistfully. "But no shit, if that gorgeous man over there decided he wanted to make it a full-time gig, I wouldn't be able to say yes fast enough."

Classic Beth, I should have known better than to ask her about no strings sex – the girl would fall in love with anyone who looked at her twice, let alone stuck his dick in her.

"Well that's not how it's going to go for me and Lukah. We're sleeping together. He's hot. It's fun. End of story."

"You're so wrong and you don't even realise it yet. This is the best."

"Seriously? *As if.* Does Lukah strike you as a relation-ship kind of guy? Even if I wanted to get serious – which I don't – he'd never be up for it. He's a player, he sleeps around."

"Is he though?"

"Is he *what*?"

"Sleeping around? Because Griff said he hasn't been with anyone but you since you guys hooked up."

I roll my eyes. "It's been what? Two weeks? Whoop-de-fucking-do."

"Two weeks is a long time for a guy that looks like that and makes a living from something that involves women throwing themselves at him."

"It doesn't even matter. We're not together. Never will be."

She giggles, as though I've said something funny. "If you say so."

She strolls away, leaving me wanting to shake her.

"I *do* say so."

"We'll see," she calls over her shoulder.

I throw the last of the bread in the lake and follow her. Grumpy, because there's more truth than I'd like to admit in everything she just said, and I could deny it until I'm blue in the face, but that won't make it any less true.

I'm not in love with the guy or anything, but I'll miss him when he's gone, and that's not something I ever anticipated.

My bad mood disappears the minute I lay eyes on Lukah. He and Griff are in stitches, laughing about something.

Damn, he looks so handsome when he's laughing, he gets sweet little indents in his cheeks, and his bright blue eyes come alive.

He's stripped off his shirt to catch some sun, and my eyes linger on each and every one of his defined abs. They contract and relax as he laughs, holding my attention.

I've never been as attracted to a guy I'm having sex with as I am to Lukah. Probably something to do with the fact that none of my previous partners have ever had a body like that.

He turns those eyes on me, his stare lingering on my face before running down the length of my body.

I shudder.

Damn him.

He's too good at this game. He knows exactly how to tempt me, and he can do it without even touching me, or saying a single word.

All of a sudden, I wish I'd blown Beth off so I could be alone with him. So not only am I lying to myself about

Lukah, I'm now a terrible friend too. Not to mention a wannabe exhibitionist.

I haven't had sex in a park before, but it's now right at the top of my list.

"You look hungry for something," Lukah says.

I lift my stare from his torso, to his face. He's smiling smugly like he can read my mind.

"I *am* hungry," I reply, dropping down to the blanket he's laid out.

"Grapes?" he offers, smirking.

I shake my head.

"Sandwich?"

"Nope."

He beckons me closer with his finger and I go, eager to hear whatever dirty thing he wants to whisper in my ear.

"Do you want me to fuck you right here on this blanket, jailbait?" he rasps, low enough for only me to hear.

I shake my head.

"No?" he questions.

I shake my head again. "I said I was *hungry*." I purr seductively, "that usually requires something to go in my *mouth*."

He groans, drags me against his body and rolls his weight on top of mine.

"You keep that up and I'll get arrested for indecent exposure."

"Don't talk smack if you can't back it up." I giggle.

"Noted," he mutters before crashing his lips to mine.

———

THERE'S a soft tap on my door and I grin.

I bet him he couldn't stay away from me all night and it looks like I'm about to win that bet.

I pause my movie and call softly, "Come in."

The lights are out, but I can make out his broad shoulders and narrow waist in the dim glow of the tv screen.

He shuts the door behind him and pads over to my bed, sliding into the sheets without bothering to wait for an invitation.

"I win." I giggle as he wraps his arms around my middle and breathes me in.

"I don't give a shit," he replies as he peppers kisses to my bare shoulder. "This is a pretty good prize for losing."

He kisses my forehead and grabs the remote from on top of the covers. "What are we watching?"

"It's a chick flick, you won't like it."

"I'll be the judge of that."

"Alright," I concede, wiggling in his arms so I can see the screen.

He hits play and we watch in silence, only he's not watching the screen at all, he's watching me.

"You're missing it," I whisper, when I catch his eye.

"It's cute that you think I give a fuck."

"Why'd you come in here if you were just going to ignore it?"

"Because *you're* in here, and I'm a smart guy."

When he says stuff like that, it's too easy to imagine that this is the real thing, that we could be something more than just sex.

"Smart you reckon?"

"Smart enough to get you to bend at my will."

I scoff. "I do *not* bend."

"Oh, you bend alright, babe," he drawls, his hand finding bare skin on my hip.

"You've got it all wrong… *I've* got *you* wrapped around *my* little finger, trouble."

He chuckles, his fingers travelling lower. "You think?"

"I *know*," I whisper, the movie forgotten.

"I need to tell you something," he says as he tugs at my underwear, the band snapping back against my skin.

"What's that?"

My heart thumps in my chest. I have a feeling I know what he's going to say. He's looking at me with a look in his eyes that I can only place as adoration.

"I think this is more than–"

He's interrupted by a loud banging on my bedroom door.

I still, listening, just in case I somehow imagined the loud noise.

The banging goes again, this time with my name being muttered along with it.

My blood runs cold. It's *Rick's* voice, outside my door, just before midnight.

Nothing good is going to come from this situation, I can feel it.

"Hide," I hiss at Lukah.

I can just make out his expression in the low light, and he looks like he's about to explode.

"He so much as lays a finger on you, and I'll kill him," he whispers, "I swear to god, Margot, I won't let him hurt you, secret be damned."

My heart leaps at the protective edge to his voice as he jumps off the bed and positions himself so he'll be behind the door when I open it.

I take a deep, steadying breath and climb to my feet to get the door.

I open it slowly, still hopeful that I imagined the entire thing, but I haven't got that kind of luck.

Rick is on the other side, unstable on his feet.

Drunk. Again.

He's a real hypocrite actually, hounding Lukah about his drinking, when he's no better himself.

I swallow the lump in my throat.

"Rick?"

He's been staring at me since I opened the door, but it's like his eyes are blurry, like he's not really seeing me.

He sways as he tries to focus on me.

"Margot," he finally says.

"Are you okay?"

He grins, wide and lazy. "Just fine."

"Was there something you needed?"

"I... um..."

He wobbles as he takes a step forward.

I'm gripping the edge of the door and I feel Lukah's fingers lightly brush mine, a silent show of support.

"I... wanted... to... to say sorry."

Relief floods through me. He's here to apologise.

"Okay."

He steps forward again, more coordinated this time, less shaky.

"You're a beautiful woman," he says as his eyes really focus on me.

That's not exactly what I had in mind when he mentioned the word 'sorry', but it's still an upgrade from the predator outside the bathroom the other day.

I narrow the gap of my open door. "Um thanks, I think I might call it a night now."

"You want some company?"

Jesus.

So much for an improvement. He's a complete asshole creep.

I don't need to see Lukah to know he's furious. I can feel the anger radiating from him. I can picture his face, the way his fists will be clenched at his sides.

"I'm good. You should go to bed. Goodnight, Rick." My tone is as final as I can muster given the way I'm freaking out.

I go to push the door shut, but his foot is there, forcing it back open. "What's the matter? One Andrews man enough for you?" he drawls.

I feel my mouth fall open in shock.

He sneers at me, his hand landing on my upper arm in a gesture I'm sure he means to be seductive, but only makes my skin crawl.

"Let go," I whisper.

His grip tightens.

"Let. Go," I repeat.

Those two words must have been Lukah's limit, because before I can even blink, I'm behind his body, the door slamming violently against the wall and my arm throbbing from where Rick grasped it.

Rick stumbles back, shock written on his face until he figures out who's standing in front of him.

"You touch her like that again, and I'll fucking kill you," Lukah sneers.

He might be on my side, protecting me, but I'm scared shitless. I've never heard a sentence so menacing.

I don't know if Rick is stupid, or just has no fear, because he laughs. He fucking laughs. "I *knew* you couldn't keep your dick away from her."

"That's real god damn rich coming from you, old man."

"She wants me."

"Like fuck she does."

"I've seen her prancing around in those revealing outfits."

Jesus. I have been doing that, but no way in hell was it for *his* benefit. It was for Lukah – everything is for Lukah.

I feel bile in my throat. Surely Rick's not that delusional. He can't seriously think I'd be interested in him, even in the slightest. The idea is repulsive. He's my mum's husband, he's old *and* he's a total pervert.

"She's just like the last one, boy, not my fault you can't keep a woman happy."

I have no idea what they're talking about, but now isn't really the time for questions.

Lukah closes the gap between them and his fist connects with Rick's jaw. Rick doesn't even see it coming, he's too drunk, too sloppy.

He stumbles back, falling into a wall with a loud thud.

"Stay the fuck away from her," Lukah bellows, his chest heaving as he stands over his father. He strikes him again, this time in the nose and blood spurts all over the plush, white carpet.

"You little fucking prick," Rick moans.

I run to Lukah before he can hit him again, gripping his biceps and trying to pull him away.

He fights against me, but he doesn't want to shake me off, not really.

I place a kiss to the middle of his shoulder blades. "Shhh, c'mon, that's enough... he's not worth it," I soothe.

"He has to pay."

"He's paying, please, Lukah," I beg, "no more, I'm okay. I just need *you*."

I might have intended to say it for his benefit, to make him stop, but it's true – I need *him*.

He relaxes into my touch, my words calming him.

A light comes on from upstairs and my mum appears on the staircase in her pyjamas, blinking drowsily until she takes in the scene in front of her.

"What the hell is going on here?" she demands, rushing to Rick's side.

I think it's pretty fucking obvious. Rick is clutching his nose, bleeding, and Lukah is shirtless, his hands splattered with his father's blood.

"Did *you* do this?" She glares at Lukah as she tries to stop the blood gushing out of Rick's nostrils.

"You bet I did."

Mum gets to her feet and takes a step in our direction, her gaze finally landing on me as she takes in the way I'm wrapped around Lukah.

"What the hell is going on here, Margot?"

I've never seen my mum so angry. She's shaking.

I open my mouth to speak, but nothing comes out.

"I'll fucking tell you what happened, he–"

"Lukah," I whisper, cutting him off.

He turns slowly, completely ignoring my mum as he faces me.

I shake my head. "Not now."

I can't tell her this, not yet. I can't destroy her hopes, her dreams, her *marriage*, not at midnight, on Christmas eve.

He searches my face, confused.

"*Please*," I beg.

He drops his head in disappointment, and I don't blame him.

"It was nothing," I say to my mum, my eyes never leaving Lukah's.

He slides his hands from my shoulders to my wrists before taking my hands in his. "*Jailbait.*"

"I know," I whisper. "Just not right now, *please.*"

Disappointment again.

"Get out of my house you little fucking asshole," Rick sneers, spitting blood.

My mum rushes back over to him, offering him her hands to help him up. "Oh my gosh, are you okay?" She fusses over him.

"I'm fine," he snaps.

He takes a step towards Lukah, and I rush in front of him on instinct, pressing my back against his bare front, holding him back. I'm not worried about Rick hurting him, in fact, it's the total opposite.

One push from his dad, and he'll crack. I might not be able to stop him a second time.

His warm skin meets mine, and I feel his breath at my neck.

"*Margot*," Mum says, shocked. "What is going on here?"

"I'll tell you what's going on here, sweetheart, I found the little prick in your daughter's room, and then he punched me."

"*What?*" Mum breathes. "You two? *Together?*"

I don't know why she's so shocked – she called it from the start.

"Fuck you, lying prick," Lukah sneers.

My mum is looking at me like I kicked her puppy. I hate that look in her eyes. I've let her down. I've never been anything but completely honest with her – it's always just been the two of us, but things have changed. She's changed, and so have I.

"Enough," I say, to everyone.

I can't take much more of this.

I don't know if I can take any more disappointment.

Not from Lukah, not from my mum.

I need a minute.

I turn on my heel and run back to my room. Lukah doesn't say a word, just follows me.

17

Lukah

"Jailbait," I plead as she throws herself on the bed, burying her face in the covers.

I lock the door behind me. I doubt that my asshole dad or her naive mother are going to follow us in here, but I'd rather be safe than sorry. I'll lose control if I'm pushed any further.

"What the hell just happened?" she asks, her voice muffled.

I cross the room and sink down next to her, dragging her up into my lap.

She weaves herself around me, burying her face into the crook of my neck.

"I'm so sorry, Margot," I murmur as I stroke her hair.

"It's not your fault."

I know it's not, rationally; I do. But I provoked him. I

played my part in this. I showed him my cards when I should have kept them close to my chest.

"He's only doing it to get at me."

"I think he's doing it because he's a sleazy old man that wants to have his cake and eat it too."

That's part of it too, undoubtably.

"I don't understand," she says suddenly, my words sinking in. "How would coming on to *me*, get to *you*?"

I brush her hair out of her face and kiss the tip of her nose. "He can see this between us. He wants to hurt me by taking you."

"That's stupid, *and* disgusting, why would he think that would work?"

I sigh, deep. "Because it's worked before."

I don't want to get into this, relive the past, but I owe it to her. Even if I haven't told her yet, I want something more than sex with her. Something *more* has to start with no secrets, or it would be doomed from the start.

"*What*?"

"He slept with my girlfriend. We were high school sweethearts and all that shit, and he reached out and took her."

"*Lukah*." She gasps.

"Cheated on my mum with a teenager."

She gasps again. "*No*. Your poor mum, poor *you*. No wonder you hate him so much."

"And he hates me because I told mum, and she left him. Men like my father think they have the right to take whatever they want. He thought he was entitled to both."

"He's an asshole, plain and simple."

"Yet... you didn't tell your mum?"

I get it – it won't be easy, but it has to be done.

"I will, I... I just have to figure out a way that it won't break her heart."

"It's only going to break her heart more, the longer she stays."

"I know," she whispers. "I'm sorry."

I kiss the top of her head. "I was trying to tell you something earlier."

"I know," she whispers, her chin dropping to hide her eyes from me.

I hook my finger under and bring her back up so we're staring at one another. "I like you, Margot."

"I like you too," she replies, too quickly.

I shake my head, my focus never wavering. "You know that's not what I mean. I'm falling for you. Hard. I've never met anyone like you, jailbait."

"Stop making me forget that we hate each other," she whispers, her voice pained.

I grip her chin. "I *never* hated you."

"But that's our thing."

"No. Our thing is me driving you crazy and you wanting me anyway."

I'm right, I know I am. she just can't admit it.

She got an idea in her head about me the first time we met, and no matter what I do or say, that image she's painted is still there in the back of her mind. Not that I can exactly blame her for that. It was one hell of a first encounter.

"You don't want me, trouble, not really," she whispers.

"You're wrong."

"You're not the guy I'm looking for."

"You're a dreamer, jailbait. What? Are you looking for some kind of Superman to swoop in and save you?"

"So what if I am?"

"Look around, Margot, I *am* your Superman."

"You don't have a cape," she whispers, her voice cracking, hurting herself and me in the process.

"You're really going to pull this shit?" I ask, my voice gruff, thick with emotion.

"I'm not pulling anything. I'm just trying to be honest."

"Then start by being honest with yourself."

"I am."

"Really? So out there with your mum, that look of shame on your face when she figured out we were together? That's you being honest? You not telling her what her good-for-nothing husband did? More honesty?"

She slides off my lap, and I get to my feet, pacing the room back and forth.

I know I'm losing it, but I can't help it. This fucking hurts.

I put myself on the line, for the first time since my heart was crushed all those years ago, and this is what happens. She denies me.

The worst part is, I know she'll regret it.

She thinks I don't know her, don't see her, but she's so wrong. I see every part of her. I see the way she sings songs under her breath, making up lyrics when she doesn't know the real ones, I see how she only like's eating cheese from the block when it's first opened... I see the way she loves, hard and completely. The way I know she loves me – the same way I love her.

Fuck, there it is, I'm in love. I love her.

I'm eyeballs-deep in the very thing I've tried so hard to avoid.

"I love you," I blurt out.

She stares up at me, her eyes wide, unblinking.

"Wha– what?"

"I love you. I want you. I *need* you, jailbait."

"I... I..." she stammers.

"Come with me. Let's get the fuck out of here and never come back."

"I *can't*," she whispers.

"You can." I drop to my knees in front of her, clasping her hands in mine. "There's no such thing as can't, remember?"

She shakes her head, her eyes glassing over.

"Look me in the eyes and tell me you don't feel the same way."

"*Lukah*..." She tries, but she can't do it, she can't meet my stare.

I rest my head in her lap, just breathing her in.

"Why are you doing this?" she whispers. "You saw my mum's reaction; *nobody* wants us to be together."

"*I* do."

"It's not enough."

"It's more than enough. Come with me."

"I can't just leave in the middle of the night. I can't do that to my mum."

"We can come back for her – tell her what Rick is really like."

"I can't," she repeats, and this time I really hear her.

It's not that she can't – she *won't*.

She *won't* choose me.

I nod, get to my feet and leave through her door for the last time, leaving my heart in there with her.

———

Griff only takes one look at me before cussing under his breath and opening the door wider to let me in.

I drop my bag to the floor and then just stand there, lost for what to do next.

He points at the couch. "Sit."

I comply.

I know I look like shit. I feel like shit.

I feel like someone has punched me directly in the chest and out the other side, taking my insides with it.

This is the worst. It's worse than my dad screwing my girlfriend, because I had someone to blame for that, but this, there's no one to blame here.

I can blame Margot for not wanting me, hell, if I was a chick, I wouldn't want me either, not for more than one night.

I'm a walking cliché. I scream 'unavailable', yet, I expected her to just believe otherwise.

It doesn't matter how real I was being, or how fucking deep these feelings go – so deep they're threatening to break me – it's not enough. It probably never will be.

I'm not that guy – not the one for her, and that breaks me.

Griff hands me a beer, and I don't even know what time it is, or what he was doing before I got here, but I'm grateful for it.

"What happened?" he asks after I've drained half the bottle.

I shake my head. "Don't want to talk about it."

"Where's Margot?"

"Home," I reply sharply.

He's quiet for a bit, just watching me drink and nursing a bottle of his own.

"You got any more of those?"

"Stupid question," he replies as I get to my feet, cross the room to the fridge and bring half a dozen more back with me.

"Alright then." He nods, seeing where this is going.

"Don't want to talk, doesn't mean I can't drink."

"Because that sounds like a fantastic idea," he drawls.

"Got a better one?"

He raises his brows at me, before shaking his head. "You do know it's Christmas day, right?"

I shrug. Guess it's after midnight then.

I don't give two shits about Christmas. Maybe I would if she was with me, but she's not and that just fucking hurts like hell.

I pop the top off another beer and down it just as fast as the first one.

"You don't have to stay up with me," I tell him as I reach for my third.

He lifts his feet to the coffee table, and crosses them at the ankles as he settles in. "Not like I sleep at night anyway."

I nod. Thankful for his company, but not willing to say the words out loud.

I get through another couple of beers and he goes to get some more from the fridge.

"You didn't do something stupid and fuck it up did you?" he eventually asks, like I knew he would.

I don't need to question what he's referring to; we've been friends long enough to wind up on the same wavelength.

"Define 'stupid'," I drawl, the alcohol settling in my veins and loosening my tongue.

"Dude."

"I know."

I don't know how many more beers I down, or when I fall asleep, but I wake to Griff snoring in his chair and the harsh sunlight blinding me through the window.

"Merry fucking Christmas," I grumble.

18

Margot

I wake up Christmas morning with a pounding head and red-rimmed eyes from crying all night. Well I don't actually wake up, given that I never went to sleep, but the sentiment is the same.

It's Christmas morning, a day that I love, and I just wish I could pull the covers over my head and disappear.

Things are bound to be beyond awkward between me, my mum and Rick this morning, but that's not what kept me awake well into the wee small hours.

That was all Lukah.

The look in his eyes when he asked me to go with him, the softness in his tone when he said he loved me, the way I literally saw his heart break when I turned him down.

I don't know why I didn't go.

As much as I hate to admit it, I'm feeling things for him too. Things that have no place between stepsiblings, and certainly no place between me and a guy like him, but I can't fight it anymore.

He makes my heart speed up to a gallop in my chest... he makes me want to run away with him.

He makes being bad seem like such a good idea.

Lukah Andrews is everything I never knew I wanted, and everything I can't have because loving him doesn't change a thing.

His dad is still married to my mum. He's still my stepbrother. He's still a bright red flag.

I groan as I hear my mum playing Christmas music on the sound system downstairs.

I might be twenty-three years old, but every year, we do Christmas the same way; carols playing on repeat and a stocking stuffed with gifts.

I think it's her way of trying to make up for the fact that I never had any siblings growing up. It's always just been me and her and that's all I've ever needed.

Until now.

My body aches for Lukah and my mind misses him even more. It's only been a few hours, but the distance between us is crippling. I know he's gone. I gave in at about three in the morning and went to his bedroom, but all his stuff was gone. *He* was gone.

He's probably halfway back to law school by now, and I don't know how on earth to reach him.

I never even got his cell number, and I can't exactly ask his dad where to find him.

The arrogant prick doesn't even know a thing about his own son.

I sit up, rub my eyes, and decide that I should just get this over and done with.

I'll go downstairs, open a few gifts, eat whatever I can

stomach and then crawl back into bed to feel miserable for the foreseeable future.

Breaking my mum's heart will have to wait for another day. I can't do that to her on her favourite day of the year, not when I've already proceeded to break two hearts in the last few hours, one of them being my own.

The idea of sitting across the table from Rick makes me want to put my head through a wall, but I'll do it for my mum.

I pull on my robe and slip out of my door, the carols increasing in volume as I make my way downstairs.

Mum is down there, swaying to the music and rummaging around under the tree, amongst the presents that have mostly all been wrapped and put there by her.

My heart drops when I think about the gift under there for Lukah, the one I went out and bought a few days ago, the one that I'll probably never get to give to him.

"Go-go. Merry Christmas!" She beams as she sees me, and I'm not sure what alternate universe I've slipped into, but it's as though last night never happened as she crosses the room and pulls me into a hug. "Rick is making waffles."

I almost gag at the mention of his name, but I stop myself.

That will only hurt my mum.

"Come on, come and open your stocking."

I let her lead me to the couch where I sit, numb, as she passes me the red stocking with my name stitched on the front.

I start opening the gifts; makeup, socks, soap, earrings, new pyjamas... all the usual suspects are here, and every other year, these things would bring a smile to my face, but today I can't muster even one.

The weight on my shoulders is heavy, the burden pressing down on me.

I wish Lukah was here.

I know he'd rather be anywhere but in this apartment, but it's just occurred to me that he was here for me. It was all for me.

"Do you like them?" Mum asks, a hopeful smile on her face.

"I love them, thank you." I give her a small smile as I set the pile of things aside. I take a deep breath. "Mum, can we talk about last night?"

She winces, and I feel terrible for bringing it up, but all the Rick stuff aside, I know I hurt her by keeping her in the dark about Lukah and me, and I want to make things right.

"Let's talk tomorrow," she suggests.

"I'd really like to get it off my chest."

She nods, fiddling with a torn piece of wrapping paper.

"I'm really sorry that you found out about Lukah and me the way you did. It wasn't that I wanted to keep it from you... but it's a weird situation, you know?"

"If by weird, you mean completely inappropriate, then yes, I *do* know."

"*Mum.*" I balk, shocked by the venom in her tone.

"What? Did you think I was going to give you my blessing? That I was going to support the two of you?"

"You're making it sound like incest or something, for the love of god, he's not my brother, mum, he's your brand-new husband's son, and frankly, I think if he could shake that title, he would."

She gets to her feet, rearranges her face into a fake smile and looks right at me. "We're not discussing this now. He's gone, that's the main thing. I'm going to go help Rick."

I blink, unmoving as she disappears into the kitchen. I don't know who that woman just now was, but it sure as hell wasn't the mother I've known my whole life. The one who would do anything for me, support me through thick and thin.

I brush a tear from my cheek.

I've never felt this alone.

I want to run upstairs and call Beth, but I don't want to ruin her day, and I don't want to let Rick win. I don't want him to break me the way he broke Lukah.

I walk on shaky legs to the tree and rummage around, looking for the gift I got my mum. I find it as she walks back into the room, Rick's arm around her.

"Here," I say as I thrust the gift in her direction.

She makes a fuss, half hugging me as I look anywhere but at Rick.

I feel sick to my stomach as he catches my eye. "Merry Christmas," he says, his eyes assessing me.

He's got a bruise on his jaw and another across his nose from where Lukah hit him.

"You too," I mumble.

I watch as Mum carefully opens the paper, folding it up after she's undone the tape.

I wish she'd hurry the hell up. I just want to get out of here.

"Oh, it's beautiful, sweetie, thank you." She gushes as she holds up the silk, floral robe to show Rick.

He nods and smiles in all the right places.

Snake.

She fishes out another couple of gifts from under the tree, passing some to me and some to Rick.

I see the poorly wrapped gift that Lukah got for my mum. It's clearly labelled, but she skips right past it like it's not even there.

"Who's this one for?" She picks up a small box and turns it over. "Jailbait," she reads aloud.

I snag it from her hands, my heart pounding as I rip off the paper, feeling the most alive I have all morning.

Lukah might not be here, but this gift is from him and it's the closest I might get for a long time.

My breath gets caught in my throat as I open the velvet box and reveal the delicate, gold locket that I pointed out the day he made me go shopping with him.

I sink down to the couch, shocked.

"I can't believe he did that," I whisper to myself.

"What is it?" Mum asks.

I turn the box, to show her the gorgeous oval locket. "It's from Lukah."

Her brows shoot up in surprise.

"That little prick," Rick mutters.

That's it. That's all it takes for my already waning control to slip entirely.

"Are you kidding me?" I snap at him, flicking the lid of the box shut in the same moment. "*You're* calling *him* a prick? That's rich coming from you."

"Margot!" Mum snaps.

"Don't *Margot* me, I don't even know who you are right now, and I bet you have no idea who the hell you've married."

So much for not breaking her heart on her favourite day. I'm on a roll now and it's going to take a damn wrecking ball to stop me.

Rick's face pales, but his staunch frame doesn't falter.

"I know *exactly* who I married."

"Do you though? Do you really? Why do you think his own son punched him in the face last night?"

"Rick told me," she replies, "he told me about catching the two of you together and Lukah lashing out when he confronted him."

I huff out a humourless laugh. "Oh that's *too* good." I point at Rick. "Well played. I'll give you that. You should have been on Broadway, you're quite the actor."

"Margot, that's enough, you're being *so* rude. I don't know what's got into you."

Rick ignores me, turning instead to my mother. "It's okay, Kate, I told you Lukah would be a bad influence on her."

"Get fucked!" I scream, snapping completely.

Mum's jaw falls open in shock.

"I am so god damn sick of hearing you talk about him like that. He's not a bad influence, he's good, and sweet and kind and he's more of a man than you'll ever be!"

"He's cocky, arrogant and self-absorbed," Rick snaps.

"He is," I agree, still raging, "but he's not *just* those things. He's so much more and you have no idea what you've missed out on."

"What? A few strip shows? Watching him shake his dick around?" Rick challenges me.

"How about the fact that he's in law school?"

Rick balks.

"Yeah, you didn't know that did you? He only strips to pay his way. So he doesn't have to ask *you* for a cent, and you know what? I don't blame him. I couldn't think of anything worse than owing you anything."

I cross the room, purpose in my stride as I snag the gift I got for Lukah from under the ridiculously expensive tree.

I'm getting out of here, right now.

"He told you he was in law school?" Rick chuckles. "He really has got you fooled."

I turn back around, all thoughts of walking out abandoned.

"He *is* in law school. Maybe if you knew a single thing about your son, you'd know that, but I guess you burnt that bridge when you fucked his teenage girlfriend, right?"

Mum gasps, her hand flying up to her mouth.

Rick looks like he could strangle me on the spot.

"Yeah, he told me how you cheated on your wife with his girlfriend. He told me *everything*, and you know what? I can't believe he ever spoke to you again. You're a shitty father and an even worse human."

"You spoilt little–"

"Oh go fuck yourself," I cut him off.

I turn to Mum, who is now clinging onto his arm like some stupid, desperate woman.

"Lukah punched him because he came on to me," I tell her, "and it wasn't the first time. Lukah was protecting me, from *him*."

"He *wouldn't*," she breathes, still at his side.

"He did," I reply, ignoring the pain in my chest as she continues to choose him over me.

I'm her daughter. She's known me for so much longer than she's known him, but she doesn't believe me.

I don't give either of them time to say anything more, I have to get out of here before I really explode and serve my mum a few home truths that I can't take back.

They're standing there, united against me, and I can't bear to breathe the same air as them any longer.

I look down at the box in my hand as I dash up the stairs to throw some stuff into a suitcase.

I know I'm probably too late, but I have to try and find Lukah, and there's only one place I can think of to go.

I just have to find him.

He'll make this better. He'll take care of me.

He was right. He *is* my Superman.

19

———————

Lukah

"You can go hang out with your family, dude, don't let me being a miserable bastard get in the way of your Christmas."

"Are you kidding?" he asks around a mouthful of greasy bacon, "I'm all for this grinch shit. All about that life."

"Your family out of town, huh?"

"Yip," he replies, smirking.

I chuckle, then rub my pounding head.

"Why'd you let me drink so many beers?"

He holds up his hands in defence. "I'm not getting in the way of a heartbroken man trying to drown his sorrows, and besides, I passed out while you were singing *The Goo Goo Dolls* at a pitch that probably woke up dogs two towns over. I'm not responsible for anything that took place after that."

"Fuck off."

"Wish I had, would have saved my ear drums the torture."

I flip him off, and take a tentative sip of my coffee, testing out my stomach.

The last thing I need is to start puking, even though I'd deserve it after the solid attempt I made to drink my body weight in alcohol.

"I know you said you didn't want to talk about it... but, I gotta know. Margot... she didn't fall for his shit, did she?"

I lift my eyes to meet his and shake my head.

She might have shot me down, but there's no way in hell she'd ever fall for my dad's 'charms'.

"I knew I liked her for a reason," he says, relieved.

"Me too." I huff. "Didn't stop him from trying it on anyway though."

"He didn't forc–"

"No," I cut him off. "I was there to get in his way. He barely laid a finger on her."

"So, I guess the sister fucker cat is out of the bag then?"

"It sure fucking is." I run my hand through my hair. "But that's the least of my worries, bro, I punched my dad in the face, told Margot I loved her and then got shot down. Now I'm spending Christmas alone with you."

He chokes on the mouthful of coffee he just took.

He coughs and splutters, his eyes wide. "Did you just say you *love* her?"

"I don't want to talk about it."

"Well you can kiss my nut sacks; we're talking about it. You can't drop something like that and then go quiet."

"What are you going to do? Tea bag me until I talk?"

"You'd like that, wouldn't you?" He waggles his brows at me.

"Dude. I'm too hungover for this."

He chuckles and then groans. "Me too."

"I think it's the real deal with her," I say after a few beats of silence.

His expression is one of sympathy. "She doesn't feel the same way?"

"I thought she did. I really thought we had something, but she just sees the stripper, the *playboy*. She'd never take a guy like me seriously."

"She's not your dad, LA, I've seen the look in her eye when she watches you."

"Me too, but I must have misjudged it."

There's a knock at the door and Griff jumps up. "That'll be the pizza I ordered."

"*How*? It's like ten in the morning. On Christmas. Where'd you even find a delivery place?"

"A magician never reveals his secrets," he calls out.

I chuckle into my coffee as I hear him opening the door and talking to the poor bastard he's probably going to tip like a tight ass.

"What flavour did you get?" I ask as I hear footsteps behind me. I could go a few slices, anything to soak up some booze.

Griff clears his throat, and I turn, but it's not him my eyes find, it's *her*.

"Maybe we were right after all," he says.

"*Jailbait*," I breathe, my heart fucking aching at the sight of her.

"Hi," she says softly.

"You're here."

She shrugs.

She looks how I feel. Shitty, exhausted, *wrecked*. But somehow, still the most perfect sight in the world.

"Are you okay?" I ask. "Did something happen with my dad?"

She nods her head.

I'm out of my seat and standing before her in a flash. "Are you okay?" I ask again.

She shakes her head, her bottom lip quivering as tears threaten.

"Shit, come here." I wrap her in my arms, and she clings onto my shirt like her life depends on it. There it is, that trust again.

There's not a lot in the world that can make me feel this good about myself but having her trust me is definitely one of them. Makes me feel like I'm worthy of it.

It doesn't matter that she doesn't feel the same way about me as I do her, or that I wish more than anything that she did, right now she needs me, and I'll be there for her.

"You want to tell me what happened?"

She nods, her face buried in my chest.

I scoop her up and carry her back out into the living room, sitting us both down on the couch.

My eyes drift around the room as I rub her back, and that's when I see them. Her bags by the door. Two huge suitcases.

I don't want to let myself get excited, but it's hard.

"Jailbait, why do you have bags?" I ask carefully.

She looks up at me, her dark eyes rimmed with tears, but her lips curving up slightly.

"You told me we could leave and never go back," she whispers. "If I'm not too late, I'd really like to take you up on that offer."

My heart is jackhammering in my chest, pounding against my ribs with such force that I'm worried it might leap right out.

I need to chill. Wanting to leave doesn't mean that she wants to be with me. I can't get ahead of myself. I need the whole story.

"What happened?" I question, the pad of my thumb skating across her cheek, wiping away a stray tear.

"I just couldn't hold it in anymore. My mum was acting like nothing happened, falling all over Rick and fake smiling... it made me sick. The straw that broke the camel's back was when I opened the necklace..."

"You opened the necklace?"

She reaches up, cupping my jaw in her hands, and that's when I see it – right there around her neck.

"I can't believe you got it for me."

"It was the one you wanted, right?"

She nods. "Yes. I love it."

I shrug. "It was no big deal."

"It's a very big deal," she whispers, tugging my face down to hers to kiss me, soft and sweet.

God, it's the best feeling in the world, but I don't want to be too hopeful. It's just a kiss. It might mean nothing to her.

I close my eyes and savour the moment, her hands on my skin, her weight in my lap, the scent of her surrounding me.

If this is the last time I'm going to get to be near her, then I don't want to forget a single part of it.

"I told my mum what he did."

My lids spring open. "I thought you wanted to wait."

"I did." She sighs. "But then he started insulting you, and I couldn't stop, I lost it. I screamed, I swore, I lost the plot, I just couldn't let him talk about you like that, it was so wron–"

I cut her off, smashing our lips together again.

She got into it with my dad, over me. She was *defending* me. I can't remember the last time someone did that.

"I don't think I'm going to be invited back next Christmas," she whispers when I pull away, sucking in air.

"You think your mum will still be with him next Christmas?" I ask, surprised.

Her eyes glass over again, and I can see how much she's hurting. "She didn't believe me. She believes him."

"Oh, jailbait," I breathe, wrapping her up tighter.

"Why would she believe him over me?"

Pain.

Broken.

Hurt.

"Because love makes people stupid, baby, really fucking stupid."

"I guess I can't really judge her." She tips her head back, seeking out eye contact. "Love is making me stupid too."

20

———

Margot

"Wʜᴀᴛ ᴀʀᴇ ʏᴏᴜ sᴀʏɪɴɢ?" he asks, his expression hopeful, wary, and terrified all rolled into one.

"You know what I'm saying."

"I... I'm–"

"For a law student, you're not very smart," Griff bellows from wherever he must be eavesdropping from, "she's telling you she loves you, you big dummy."

I burst into laughter at the same time that Lukah yells, "fuck off, Griff."

He turns back to me, his expression soft. "Is that what you're telling me, jailbait? You love me?"

I look right into those magnetising blue eyes and know I made the right choice by coming here on a whim to find him.

He's *everything*.

"I love you even when I hate you," I tell him. "Even

when I want to wipe that cocky smirk clean off your face, you still get the better of me. You're my Superman."

He beams wide, those perfect pearly white teeth on display.

"Even if I'm a stripper?" he teases.

"Yeah… *look*, we might need to talk about that."

He chuckles. "Buzz kill."

"Floozy."

"Bore."

"Show pony."

"*Mine.*"

I scoff, trying to hide the effect that one word has on me. I feel it all the way down to my stomach.

"You were always mine, jailbait," he murmurs as his fingers caress my neck.

"What if I didn't want to be yours?"

"Bad fucking luck."

Doesn't feel much like bad luck to me; feels like the grand prize.

He brings his mouth to mine, brushing his lips in a taunting, teasing way that drives me crazy.

I deepen the kiss, groaning when I feel his tongue slip into my mouth.

"I missed you," I murmur against him.

"I missed you too."

"You two are pathetic, it's been less than twelve hours," Griff calls out.

"Stop fucking listening in, dude, it's weird."

"I was waiting for my invite for a group hug."

I giggle, resting my head against Lukah's strong shoulder. "Is he always like this?"

"*Always.*"

"Lucky you don't live around here then, huh?"

Sadness flashes in his eyes. "I live hours away."

I nod. "I know."

"But we can do this, I've only got to finish this year and then–"

"Shut up. I'm coming with you."

"*What*?" he asks on a deep exhale.

I feel myself blush. "I mean, if you want me to."

"Are you fucking serious?" He grins.

I hitch my thumb over my shoulder. "I didn't pack the bags for nothing."

"What about your job?"

I shrug. "I'll find another one."

"What about your mum?"

I'll miss my mum, truly, but until she comes to her senses, I'm not sure I can have her in my life the same way she always has been.

"I think it might be time for us to make our own decisions."

He's staring at me in wonder. "You're seriously going to drop everything and follow me across the country?"

"Love makes people stupid, remember?" I grin.

I shriek as he jumps to his feet with me still cradled against him, swinging me around.

"God, I love you," he says as he presses his forehead against mine.

"I know you do."

"Is this present for me?" Griff asks, interrupting the moment as he picks up and shakes the gift I brought for Lukah.

Lukah groans. "I should have got a hotel room."

"I wouldn't have found you in a hotel," I point out.

"*Still.*"

Griff shakes the package and I laugh. "Sorry, Griff, it's for my boyfriend."

Griffon pouts.

"Boyfriend, you reckon?" Lukah rasps in my ear.

I can tell he likes the way that sounds, his voice is rough and sexy.

"You bought me jewellery. If I remember correctly, that's part of the boyfriend package."

"What else is part of the boyfriend package?" he growls.

"You'll see." I smirk, running my tongue over my lips seductively.

"Fuck presents, show me now."

"Uh, guys, I'm still here," Griff interrupts.

"I'm well aware." Lukah sighs, pulling back and taking my hand in his. "Give me that."

Griff tosses it across the room – luckily, it's not breakable – and then drops onto the couch to watch Lukah open it.

He eyes me curiously as he tears the paper off.

"It's for when you're a big-shot lawyer," I say, before he can comment.

He runs his fingers over the soft brown leather of the briefcase, pausing to linger on the 'L.A.' that I had engraved into the side.

"This must have cost you a fortune," he murmurs, still turning it over in his hands.

"It was no big deal," I say, earning a smirk from him when he realises it's the same line he tried to use on me about the locket around my neck.

"It's incredible. Thank you."

"You're welcome."

"What's this?" He frowns as he opens it, seeing the small red pin I attached to the lining.

"It's a red flag." I giggle.

He looks at me curiously.

"Because you're the biggest red flag I've ever seen, and against my better judgement, I fell for you anyway."

He chuckles. "Smartass."

"Merry Christmas, Lukah."

"Merry Christmas, jailbait."

———

"Are you sure?" I whisper as we linger outside the door of Rick and Mum's apartment.

"You think I'd let him come near you?"

"It's not about Rick."

It *is* about Rick, but not in the way he's thinking. I know Lukah would never let his father touch me, not ever again. But that's not what worries me – an assault charge does.

I shift my weight from foot to foot, nerves fluttering in my belly.

I left here in such a rush that I didn't even pack all of my stuff, and Lukah put the idea in my head that we could get out of here first thing tomorrow, and road trip our way to my new home – so I need to collect the last of it.

Really, I think he just wants to give one last 'fuck you' to his dad and my mum by showing them a united front, but that's okay with me. I'll never keep Lukah a secret, ever again.

He smirks at me. "Don't you trust me, jailbait?"

"Oh, I trust *you*, but I *don't* trust that devious glint in your eye."

"Smart girl."

He pounds his fist against the door, and I hold my breath, waiting to see who will come to answer it.

I threw my key in a fit of rage when I bolted out of here earlier. If I still had it, I'd probably have let myself in and taken my chances sneaking upstairs to grab my stuff.

The door swings open and it's my mum on the other side.

"Go-go," she breathes, her relief obvious until she takes in the man behind me with his arms wrapped protectively around my waist.

"What are *you* doing here?" she says, her tone heavy, wary.

"I just want to pack the last of my stuff," I tell her, even though she was speaking to Lukah, not me.

"Where are you going to go? You haven't got a place yet, just stay a while longer."

There're hints of my mum in there, the concern in her voice – but it's vastly outweighed by the fact that she's clearly not planning to go anywhere herself, and more than that, she wants *me* to stay here too. With *him*. Even after I've told her what he did.

"That's not happening," Lukah answers for me, mirroring my thoughts.

Mum glares at him and then shifts her focus back to me. "Is he speaking on behalf of you now?"

I sigh heavily. "You know what? Yeah. He's more than welcome to, because I know he has my best interests at heart, and because he's right. That's *not* happening."

"Are you suggesting I don't have your best interests at heart?"

I shrug. "I don't know anymore, Mum, I honestly don't know. You're different. I don't know when it happened, but a switch has flipped, and I can't say where your priorities lie."

"We just want to get her stuff and we'll be out of your hair." Lukah presses against my back, urging me forward.

Kate steps aside and lets us pass.

"Where will you go?" she asks our backs.

I turn slowly to face her, Lukah turning with me. "I'm going to go home with Lukah."

"He's your stepbrother."

I shrug. "I don't care. I love him and I'm going with him."

"Can't say I didn't see this happening."

I feel Lukah tense behind me at the sound of his father's voice.

I hear his feet approaching, passing us, but I don't look at him until he's standing next to my mother.

I don't think I've ever hated a person. Not my dad for running out on my mum when she was pregnant, not my science teacher for failing me because I chewed gum in class... not even Lukah, even when I promised him I did... but I *hate* Rick. I hate him with every fibre of my being.

He makes my skin crawl and my heart feel heavy. I can't even imagine how Lukah feels when he looks at him.

"I told you he'd be nothing but trouble," Rick mutters to my mum.

He *is* nothing but trouble, but he's *my* trouble.

"I thought you'd be too smart for his tricks, I really did," he scolds me. "You're making a mistake."

"I'm not doing this," I whisper, turning to Lukah. "I'm better than this, *we're* better than this... I'm not going another round, and you don't need any more busted knuckles."

He's still sending his dad a death glare, and I cup his face, forcing him to turn his face towards mine.

I press up on my tippy toes and kiss his lips softly. "*Please*?"

He relaxes a fraction, but he's still so tightly wound, I know he could snap at any second.

"Go pack your shit," he murmurs.

"Forget it, I can just buy new stuff."

"Fuck that."

"You'll be a rich lawyer soon, you can afford it."

That earns me a smirk.

He sighs, more tension dissipating from his broad shoulders.

"Alright, jailbait."

He takes my hand in his, grounding me, calming me, and me doing the same for him in return.

My mum and Rick are speaking, probably talking more bullshit, but I don't hear a word they say as I let Lukah lead me past them, right out the front door and out of the building, away from them and their bullshit.

It's the most freeing feeling in the world.

EPILOGUE

Lukah

"W AS THAT YOUR MUM?"

She nods, tossing her cell phone onto the bed in our tiny apartment.

A couple more months and I'll be able to afford to get us a bigger place, not that jailbait would ever complain.

I did offer to get the money by other means, but she made it very clear that the only dancing I'd be doing was for her, in private.

"She's still got her head in the sand." She sighs. "You know, I really thought when she called last week, that he'd finally pushed her past her limits, but I guess she's still hanging in there."

I carry a lot of guilt over Margot's mangled relationship with her mother, no matter how many times she tells me that it's not my fault, I still feel at least partially responsible.

If I hadn't shown an interest in Margot, my dad probably never would have either. I know that's fucked up logic, but it is what it is.

"She'll get there. Give her time."

She sighs. "I guess."

"What can I do to cheer you up?" I ask.

The corners of her mouth turn up. "I can think of a few things."

I push off the wall and prowl towards her, eating up the space between us as fast as I can.

I push her shoulders down into the mattress and lower myself on top of her. "What'd you have in mind, jailbait?"

"You know what I want."

"Tell me."

She beckons me lower with her finger, and I bring my ear to her mouth.

She nips at the lobe with her teeth, and I growl deep in my throat.

"I *want*..." she breathes heavy, her voice husky, "... no, I *need*... some Chinese food."

Fuckin' jailbait.

"Tease." I grunt, rolling off her.

She giggles, proud of herself. "Not my fault that your mind is always in the gutter, trouble."

"Can you blame me? Look at you."

She nibbles on her bottom lip, still shy when I compliment her.

I jump to my feet, take her hand and drag her up with me. "We can get you food, but I need to have a salad."

She rolls her eyes. "You're ridiculous."

I smirk as I tug her behind me, leading her out to the living room. "Don't want to look bloated for my big moment."

"I still think you're messing with me," she says as she grabs her bag and slings it over her shoulder.

I hold the door open for her and she strolls out, eying me the entire time.

I chuckle. "I'm dead serious, jailbait. Maybe you better come with me tomorrow, since you don't believe me."

"I'll do no such thing."

"Then how are you going to know if it really happens?"

She narrows her eyes at me. "You can buy me a copy of the fucking thing."

I chuckle as the elevator stops at the carpark level to let us out. "You'd think you'd be happy. I photograph really well."

She mutters something under her breath and walks ahead of me before spinning around and coming back toe to toe with me. "What made you think it was a good idea to sign up for a calendar? I mean, *c'mon*, you're smarter than that."

I chuckle, looking down at her, my wild child. "So, you *do* believe me."

She groans in frustration. "I thought maybe if I failed to acknowledge it, then it wouldn't happen."

"I guess you were wrong."

"You're such a dickhead."

I wrap my arm around her and drag her close, covering her mouth with mine.

She sighs, her heart racing.

"It's just a photo, baby."

"I know," she replies as she grips the front of my shirt. "I kinda liked keeping your sexy Santa outfit all to myself."

"That might be the sweetest thing you've ever said to me." I smirk.

"Shut up," she grumbles.

I nudge her chin, tipping her head to look at me, those pretty brown eyes meeting mine. "You own me," I promise her.

"Thousands of women will own a little part of you too after this."

"You sound jealous, jailbait."

"I *am* jealous!" she says, her voice rising.

"You're insanely fucking sexy when you're jealous."

"I'm glad you think so." She pouts.

I kiss her lips, her cheek, her nose, her eyelids until she's smiling. "I'll make you a deal, you come with me to this shoot, and I'll give you a private dance when we get home. I've been working on some new shit. I'll be their Mr. December for ten minutes; I'll be yours forever. Deal?"

"No."

She opens her mouth to argue further, but I'm not taking no for an answer. She shrieks as I pick her up, her thighs gripped in my hands and her back hitting the concrete wall of the parking garage as I pin her against it.

She gasps. "What are you doing?"

"Right here, jailbait, just try me," I warn her.

"You don't play fair," she breathes.

"Never said I would."

I thrust my hips forward and she lets out a soft moan.

"You win."

"Always do." I smirk.

ALSO BY NICOLE S. GOODIN

<u>Love like Yours Series</u>

Rushed – Book 1

Pierced – Book 2

Hunted – Book 3

Chased – Book 4

———

<u>Rock Games Novels</u>

Paper, Scissors, Rock: Vol. 1

Hide and Seek: Vol. 2

———

<u>The Heart Duet</u>

My Heart Needs

My Heart Wants

———

<u>Calendar Boys Novels</u>

Mr. January

Mr. February

Mr. March

Mr. April

Mr. May

Mr. June

Mr. July

Mr. August

Mr. September

Mr. October

Mr. November

Mr. December

ACKNOWLEDGMENTS

The songs that inspired this book: *Hands To Myself* – Selena Gomez, *Ruin My Life* – Zara Larsson, and *I Want You out of My Head* – Bitter Cane.

I can't believe it. December is done.

Twelve books, twelve months. Done and dusted.

When I decided to start this project, the end seemed like forever away, but here I am, twelve books down, and I didn't even have to pull one all-nighter. Pat on the back for me.

I can't believe it's all over!

I'm going to miss writing about a new man every month, but I have so many other exciting projects coming up too, that I can't wait to get started on.

I need to thank a few people for sticking with me this year; Stacey – who is not only my editor, but a great friend, thank you so much for all the encouragement, and for constantly supporting me. Bianca – would be lost without you sliding into my PM's on the daily, even if we rarely have any type of constructive conversation, haha!

MV Ellis, or do I write your real name? Well I've made that awkward now, let's stick with MV – I'm not even sorry, can't even say #sorrynotsorry, because I'm not sorry about being not sorry, you're stuck with me. Deal with it. Renee – I can always rely on you to encourage me to buy stock images that I don't need. Don't know what I'd do without you... probably have better self-control.

Everyone that has read all those books, or any of them! Thank you so much, your support means so much to me and without you all reading, there wouldn't be much point.

My editors, Stacey and Trina – I know you two are going to miss my monthly stories as much as I am, but I've got more coming for you guys next year, just maybe not twelve of them!

My reader group, my street team, and all the bloggers who have shown me so much support and loyalty, thank you all from the bottom of my heart. I really am so grateful for everything that you do for not only my writing career, but for me personally too.

Thank you for reading Mr. December. Lukah and Margot were so much fun to write, and I hope you enjoyed the book! Have a very Merry Christmas and an amazing New Year!

Nicole x

ABOUT THE AUTHOR

NICOLE S. GOODIN is a romance author and mother of two from Taranaki in the North Island of New Zealand.

In mid-2015, she started to write about a group of characters who wouldn't get out of her head. Her first book, Rushed, was published in mid-2016.

Nicole enjoys long walks on the beach, pillow fights and braiding her friends' hair. She dislikes clichés, talking about herself in the third person, and people who don't understand her sense of humour.

Please feel free to contact her either via her website, email, Instagram, Twitter or on her Facebook page, she would love to hear your feedback. If you're feeling really game, you can even sign up for her newsletter.

Visit www.nicolegoodinauthor.com for more information.

UPCOMING TITLES

Cocky Hero Club Novel

Master Manipulator

———

Rock Games Novels

One For The Money

9 780099 512767